ONLY THE LONELY

Tamara von Werthern

Para-Site Publications

Only the Lonely first published in Great Britain in 2022 as a paperback original by Para-Site Publications, 117a Rushmore Road, London E5 0HA

Translated and adapted from the German novel *Ich Glaub, Es Hackt! Ein Hofheimer Lokalkrimi in der Philipp-Reihe* by Tamara von Werthern

1 edition

Copyright 2022 Tamara von Werthern

Tamara von Werthern has asserted her right to be identified as the author of this work

Editor: Robin Booth

Typesetter: Brighton Gray

Cover design: andrewdavisdesigns.co.uk

Printed in Great Britain by Mimeo Ltd, Huntingdon, Cambridgeshire PE29 6XX

ISBN: 978-0-95595-114-5

ONLY THE LONELY

TAMARA VON WERTHERN

Para-Site Publications

*For my father, the original accidental detective –
and for Maschka, of course!*

ONLY THE LONELY

PROLOGUE

I'm waiting. Sometimes I feel as if I've been waiting my whole life. Waiting for something to happen, something bigger, something important.

Waiting for you.

All this time I've been lurking in the shadows of my own life. I don't know how to grab it by the horns as others do. They know how to live, how to laugh, make friends. Things come easily to them. Maybe things just haven't gone my way. Maybe my time will come.

Watching you, I can hardly bear how full your life seems to be. How full and happy, and how unimportant I am to you. It's not fair. But I know that if I'm patient, at some point you will have used it all up. When your happiness has been spent, and your life feels just like mine, I will be there. You will see me for what I am. It will be my turn then.

Until then, I wait.

ONE
Blondes are more persuasive

Annelie checked the address her friend Laura had given her. This was it, all right. She took a moment to run her fingers over her hair, patting it down. Then, anxiously straightening her summer dress, she looked up at the house.

Her friend had spoken highly of this man. Unusual, she'd said. Some kind of minor aristocrat, someone who moved in elevated circles, was seen at parties in castles. Not your average private eye. But he lived right here in Hofheim, and she could personally recommend him.

Well, it was certainly no castle. The house she was standing in front of was, at first glance, rather ordinary: it was large and white, with a porch and a heavy wooden door. The front garden was badly overgrown, and right in the middle of it stood an old tractor, its turquoise paint flaking off over patches of rust. Despite its appearance, it was clearly still in use: there were fresh tyre tracks in the muddy ground, and great swathes of grass and other plants had been flattened. She went on past it, up to the door, and looked at the inscription on the nameplate. There it was: 'Philipp von Werthern'. That was the name Laura had given her, but alongside it was a piece of cardboard that listed several other surnames, handwritten, one of them even scribbled out. It all gave the impression of being makeshift, and not entirely trustworthy. Still, she was here now. She rang the doorbell.

There was a distant ringing inside the house. Somewhere, a dog barked. She waited. Nobody came.

Strange, she thought. If there were so many people living here, surely one of them would be at home? But there was only silence now coming from the house. How disappointing.

There was a path, she noticed, leading down a slope and to the back of the house. It wouldn't hurt to take a look. The path went down the side of the building, past several windows. She caught a glimpse of a study with a desk strewn with papers. A TV was on, blaring out a talk show to an empty room. No sign of anybody at home.

The path led to a gate, beyond which was the back garden. This too was overgrown, with a children's climbing frame to one side and, right in the middle, a motorbike and sidecar in the long grass. It wasn't the only vehicle parked here, either. There was an old Mercedes, its bonnet propped open, and someone's bottom-half sticking out of it.

Annelie put one hand on the gate and tried a tentative 'Hello?' A head shot up and banged against the underside of the bonnet. It belonged to a man in his late fifties, perhaps, in jeans and T-shirt, his clothes ripped and stained, and much of the rest of him smeared in oil and grease. On his feet was a pair of red leather clogs, and he wore wire-rimmed glasses, which he'd shoved up into his thick black hair. Next to him a golden retriever stood up out of the long grass, its tail wagging delightedly.

'I'm so sorry,' said Annelie, 'I hope you haven't hurt yourself. I'm looking for a Philipp von Werthern? I was told he lives here.'

The man came towards her, stretching out an oily hand. He had a big smile on his face, and she could just make out some friendly dimples somewhere under the grease and stubble. His teeth, in contrast, looked very white. 'That's me,' he said. 'I'm Philipp.'

Annelie was taken aback. Was this the man her friend had told her about? The minor aristocrat? The one who went dancing in castles? It seemed improbable. He looked so unlike her mental image of him that it took her a moment to regain her composure. Philipp opened the gate to let her in, and only then seemed to notice the state of the hand he was still proffering. 'Just look at me,' he said. 'I'd better go and get cleaned up. Tell you what, I'll make us some tea, and then you can tell me why you're here.'

He led her up a few steps onto a terrace, and she sat down at a trestle table with benches either side while he went into the house, accompanied by the dog. She had a moment to take in her surroundings. The tabletop was rough and grey, and there was a not-inconsiderable danger of getting a splinter from it. It was covered in crumbs and sported a few stains of dubious origin. There was a sugar bowl, a half-empty bottle of Coke, a crime novel face-down with its spine breaking into fine creases, and several glasses and mugs containing unidentifiable liquids in varying states of putrefaction. There were tomato plants growing in pots along the side of the terrace, an old stone pizza oven in one corner, and several large fridge-freezers standing about forlornly. To the left, under an awning, there was a Hollywood swing with a white-and-yellow-striped cover.

The garden beyond was, if anything, even more peculiar. There were roses growing in old metal oil canisters, and an attempt at a vegetable patch over in one corner. There, too, were the stranded Mercedes, the motorbike with the sidecar, and, at the back, a wooden structure which looked suspiciously like a horse stable. Surely, he couldn't have a horse in his garden? Behind that was an area enclosed by wire mesh, in which a dozen or so chickens were scratching and fluttering. It was altogether unlike any other garden she had come across in this neck of the woods. Hofheim was a town that prided itself on close-cropped lawns, abundant fruit trees, neat vegetables growing in rows, and flowers that were well pruned.

What, Annelie wondered, had she let herself in for?

Inside the house, Philipp was making a pot of tea, and trying to track down the cherry crumble cake he'd recently bought from Aldi. He'd scrubbed his hands and face, and though his arms were still streaked with oil, he looked slightly more presentable than before. He'd even changed into a clean T-shirt and a pair of shorts. He was, he had to admit, somewhat struck with this unexpected visitor. She belonged in the category 'rather attractive'. In fact, looking at her now through the kitchen window as she sat there on the terrace waiting for him, he thought he might even classify her as 'very attractive'. She had a pleasantly rounded face with serious eyes framed by hair that was so blonde, it made her look Scandinavian. The sun was playing on her hair, making it shine, and a soft breeze had lifted a strand that fell loosely over her face.

Philipp shook himself out of his reverie. What was he thinking? He was a man about to turn sixty, a grandfather, and this woman was probably younger than his eldest daughter. He couldn't allow himself to think like this. Many years ago, when Martha, his daughter, had been fifteen, they'd struck a deal: she was not to come home with a boyfriend who was older than him, and he in turn was not permitted to have a girlfriend younger than her. Since he'd become a dad at nineteen, the age gap wasn't enormous, but rules were rules, weren't they? Looking at this woman who'd just walked into his life through the garden gate, he wondered if it wasn't time to throw such rules on the compost heap. Besides, he felt barely any older than thirty. True, his hair was greying a little, and she probably wouldn't have given him a second look if they'd met at a party, but the fact was that she had come to his house, looking for him – who knows, maybe he stood a chance after all. It was in any case a welcome distraction on this sunny afternoon. The car could wait; he had plenty of other cars anyway.

As he came out onto the terrace – carrying the old silver tea pot, a jug of milk, two mugs and the cherry crumble cake, still in its packaging – she turned to look at him. Her eyes, he noticed, were more grey than blue, with a concentric ring of rusty orange around her left pupil. He liked the way she looked at him. He put everything down on the table, took a seat opposite her, kicked off his red Danish leather clogs and stretched his filthy toes in the summer air. The grainy concrete of the terrace floor felt pleasantly warm beneath his feet.

'Shall I just begin…' she said but stopped short when he held up his hand.

'Allow me,' he said, and leaned over to pour the tea. As he did so, she tied her hair up in a ponytail, imprisoning the rogue strand. Philipp watched it disappear with a certain regret. She really was very blonde. Maybe she *was* Scandinavian. In any case she had the cheekbones for it. He passed her a cup, and offered her the sugar bowl. When she refused it, he stirred two heaped spoonsful of sugar into his own cup, took a substantial slice of the cherry crumble cake for himself, slid the rest over to her, and settled back in his seat. Finally, his mouth full of cake, he gave her a nod.

She cleared her throat nervously, and began: 'My name's Annelie Janssen. I'm a friend of Laura's. She told me about You.' She used the formal 'You', which in German is both a mark of respect and of distance. Philipp – who found that the longer he looked at her face, the more fascinating it became – didn't like the way this 'You' gave their conversation the air of a business transaction. He held up his hand once again.

'Please,' he said, 'Don't stand on formalities. Everyone just calls me Philipp.'

Her eyes darkened slightly as she took in this new information. There seemed to be a whole weather system in those eyes, and Philipp marvelled at them.

'Thank you, Philipp,' she said, dropping her eyes. Then she looked up at him again. 'Laura said you could help me. She said you're the best private eye in the whole of Hofheim.'

Philipp nodded. To be fair, he didn't know what else he could do. He felt flattered, of course, and didn't feel there was any hurry to put her right. Strictly speaking, he was no private eye. Laura had always had a thing for exaggeration. She was an old family friend, whom he'd known all his life. Really she had been a friend of one of his sisters, but they had all played together. There was a picture somewhere of the two of them swinging colourful plastic beach spades in the sandpit in their garden. Over the years they had stayed in touch, and met up occasionally. And then he had helped her out, that time her grandmother's earrings had been stolen. He'd got them back for her, it's true, but that was more down to his connections in the so-called Hofheim underworld. It was a small town, and he knew a lot of people in it. All he'd had to do was ask around, and one of the boys who helped him with removals had given him a few tips, told him where to look. Private eye! He smiled to himself. True, he liked to have a good crime novel on the go, especially when he was on the loo, but that was about the extent of it. This Annelie Janssen or whatever her name was – perhaps she *was* Scandinavian! – must have taken Laura's praise at face value. Well, no bad thing, since it had brought her to his door.

She was looking at him now, so trustingly, with her eyes darkening to anthracite. Another sunny strand of hair had fought its way to freedom and was dancing in the breeze about her lovely face. The bronzed skin of her upper arms clinched the deal. He couldn't disappoint her, not now. It couldn't do any harm to hear what she had to say.

'So, what happened, exactly?' he asked. 'What do you need investigating?'

She stopped blowing on her cup of tea and put it down, untasted. 'I went to the police,' she said. 'They laughed me right out the door.'

'What? Laughed at you, did they?' Philipp had a long-standing feud with the Hofheim police force. More of a friendly bickering, really, but 'feud' sounded more impressive. They'd often had to come knocking at his door. Mostly it was because someone had reported that one of his cars was leaking oil again. One time it was because his horse had escaped and was trotting down the *autobahn*, threatening to cause a pile-up. Minor misdemeanours. In no way his fault. 'I don't like to hear that,' he said. '*Laughed* at you? That's not right.'

'They did,' she said. 'The officer in charge seemed to think it was hilarious. That I should even dream of reporting it! Wasting police time, he said.'

'Don't tell me. Was it a fat guy? Grey hair? Red cheeks?'

'Yes! Exactly! You know him?'

'Oh yes. His name's Schnied. Don't worry about him, he's a little bit…' Philipp tapped his index finger against his forehead to show his opinion of Hannes Schnied. 'But you were saying…'

'Yes. It's about my cat. You see, somebody must have… someone has hacked off her paw.'

Slowly, Philipp lowered his piece of cherry crumble and looked at her. 'Her paw, you say?'

'Yes. With a hacksaw. At least, I think.'

'And did you see this happen?'

Her eyes, which had been trained on him, now lost their focus and her gaze fell to the floor. She seemed to be looking inward at an image fixed in her mind. 'No, not exactly. I found her shortly afterwards.'

Philipp scratched his head. 'What makes you think it was hacked off? In my experience, when an animal loses a limb, it's usually because they've got it trapped somewhere and it gets ripped off. Or they've got into a fight with another animal. A fox. Or a dog. People don't go around hacking off cats' limbs. Not in my experience, anyway.' The question now settled, he popped a hefty piece of cherry crumble cake into his mouth.

When he looked up, he saw that Annelie's eyes were brimming with tears.

'Philipp,' she said, 'Could I ask you a favour? Would you please come back to mine? I'd feel so much better if you would.'

TWO

The case commences...
in a fine old motor car

They went in through a French window that opened onto the living room. The room felt gloomy after the bright sunlit terrace. There was a dark, heavy atmosphere, augmented by the looming presence of a very large antique oak wardrobe that took up the whole of one wall, and oil paintings in heavy gilded frames that were occupying the others. Out of one of them, a dark-haired lady peered down with a disapproving look. Annelie felt as if she had just met her boyfriend's mother for the first time and had displeased her in some way. She had the fleeting impression that she was standing in a grand and opulent castle. This illusion was shattered, however, when she noticed that, spread all over the dining table and sideboards, there was a startling profusion of coffee mugs, dirty crockery, ashtrays and half-filled glasses. In amongst it all were piles of paperwork, official-looking documents, photographs, postcards and miscellaneous till-receipts. It looked like a filing cabinet had exploded in the middle of a dinner party. Passing an open door to a black-and-white-tiled kitchen, Annelie glimpsed great towers of unwashed plates, mugs and glassware teetering on every surface.

'Looks like you had quite a party last night. Your birthday?'

Philipp laughed. 'Nothing special. Just a family meeting.' No, he had plans for his birthday. Significantly bigger plans.

'You must have a sizeable family,' she said.

He did. In fact, he had two ex-wives, four children, and six grandchildren. But this wasn't the time to go into all that. 'My cousins,' he said. 'We get together once a month. It's good to stay in touch.'

'How lovely,' she said. 'The last time I saw my cousin, I must have been ten years old.' She picked up a plate that was about to topple, and set it down on a spare corner of the table.

In truth, Philipp hadn't really noticed the state of the house. It was all quite normal to him. He had three housemates, Michi, Brian and Youssef, and none of them were that particular about household cleanliness. They'd designed a cleaning rota once, and had pinned it up in the bathroom, but it had been forgotten long ago. Besides which, the dishwasher was on the blink again, so dirty crockery was being stacked up in any available space – including inside the broken dishwasher itself – until one of the housemates felt like washing up by hand. Philipp didn't really mind. Household chaos was almost a badge of honour to him. He always felt he had more important things to do than spend his time wearing marigolds and polishing curtain rails. He'd simply made it his life philosophy to prioritise other things.

Philipp made a clicking sound with his tongue and the golden retriever jumped up from where she'd been lying, curled up in her basket, and pressed herself against his legs.

'This is Maschka, by the way.'

'Hello, Maschka.'

'Mind if she comes too? She can stay in the car.'

'I don't mind at all.' She stroked Maschka's head, and

Maschka wagged her tail appreciatively.

'Oh, and I have to stop off at the vehicle licensing office.' He fished for something that was balanced high up on a hat-shelf. It was a car number plate. He turned and smiled at Annelie. 'It shouldn't take long.'

The bright sunlight enveloped them again as they stepped outside. 'Did you come by car?' Annelie shook her head. 'No, I took the bus and walked up. I was in Hofheim anyway for some errands today.' Philipp nodded in a satisfied way, and ushered her to an MG parked at the roadside. He opened the door for her, and she had to crouch down low to slide herself into the leather seat that seemed to hover inches above the surface of the road. The steering wheel was on the right-hand side, which Annelie wasn't used to. Philipp had travelled to the UK specially to buy it. It was a fine car, in British racing green, and it had only one or two defects, so small they were hardly worth mentioning. Maschka jumped up onto the narrow shelf behind the two seats, which was just large enough for a dog of her size. With a trusting gaze, she placed her muzzle on Philipp's shoulder, and he turned the key in the ignition. At once an almighty and unhealthy sounding roar tore through the tranquil summer day. At the horrifying sound of it, Annelie gave a tiny screech.

'Just a little engine trouble,' Philipp shouted over the rattling cacophony. 'But it drives like a dream.' He pulled out, and the three of them rolled off towards town.

Philipp parked directly outside the licensing office so that he could keep an eye on things from inside. The ladies who worked there knew him well, and even kept dog treats in their desk drawers so they could spoil Maschka. The two of them were always popping in, mostly on other people's business: his love of classic cars extended to buying them on behalf of clients, often travelling far and wide to track down the right vehicle, and as part of the service he'd always make sure the paperwork was present and correct.

As he waited in line, he looked out at the blonde woman and the equally blonde dog, sitting in the MG. They looked like they belonged together. It filled him with a sudden happiness to see Annelie scratching Maschka's head and talking with her. He was already looking forward to the drive out to Langenhain, where Annelie had told him she lived. It wasn't far, just on the edge of Hofheim. The road there curved through some beautiful woodland as it wove its way towards the foothills of the Taunus Mountains, and the views were quite something. It was shady too, which would be pleasant on a day like today. He'd enjoy the drive, and if he had to listen to more nonsense about amputated cat paws, well then so be it. He would show some compassion. The woman even seemed to be good with dogs. Maybe she wasn't quite as young as she looked. With any luck, she'd be older than thirty-nine, and then nobody could possibly complain, even his eldest daughter.

'All done!' he said, returning to the car. He got in, slamming the driver's door with a crunch that made Annelie flinch. 'Sorry, it's just a bit stiff. It works fine. Nothing to worry about.' And they set off towards the town centre.

Against his expectations, Annelie didn't talk about her cat, and they had a pleasant conversation, as far as was possible over the excruciating noise of the engine. She even agreed to his suggestion that they stop off at Venezia, the ice cream parlour in the middle of town. By lucky coincidence they bumped into Thorsten, a nice young chap who was a client of Philipp's in his capacity as insurance salesman. Selling insurance had been Philipp's first 'proper' job, and he liked to do business in his own style, inviting clients to his home, plying them with tea and biscuits from his special biscuit cupboard, and, instead of drowning them in sales patter, listening to them attentively as they unfolded their entire life stories. He always found the best deals for them too, but that was by-the-by: they came to him to be listened to, and for his ready supply of biscuits. When Thorsten saw Philipp there outside Venezia with a beautiful woman beside him, it was enough to jog his memory that his home insurance needed renewing, and he made an appointment for next week, for tea and biscuits. That was exactly how Philipp liked to do business. Thorsten's admiring glance at Annelie made him a little giddy too. It wasn't often that he was in a position to be seen out and about having an ice cream with a stunning Scandinavian blonde.

The drive through shaded woodland was pleasant and the hazelnut ice cream hit the spot. Life was as it should be. From the corner of his eye, Philipp saw Annelie relax and lean her head against the leather headrest. Next to her, Maschka's snout inched slowly forwards, until she, too, rested her head on the seat. A smile crept up and crinkled his eyes as he saw Annelie putting her hand up to Maschka's head to give her another friendly scratch. Maschka twitched her nose and her dark eyes closed slowly in enjoyment of it all. She was falling head-over-heels for Annelie, that was easy to see.

Annelie's house was half-hidden behind some sad-looking plane trees. It was one half of a semi-detached house, and they had to cross a flagstone courtyard and go around the side of the house to reach the front door at the rear. 'Stay!' Philipp instructed Maschka, who was all set to follow her new best friend into the house. 'I need you there to keep an eye on the car,' he added kindly, just to give her a sense of purpose. Maschka curled herself up in Annelie's still-warm seat and watched with sad eyes as they disappeared around the corner.

At the front door, Annelie rummaged in her bag for her keys, but before she could find them the door opened abruptly and a woman wearing glasses stuck her head out.

'Ah! Frau Schmitt!' Annelie exclaimed. 'However did you know we were here?'

Philipp smiled at the woman. He suspected that the car – which in many respects was faultless – had alerted her to their arrival, but he said nothing about it.

'This is Frau Schmitt,' said Annelie. 'She does the cleaning.'

Philipp shook the woman's slightly clammy hand and introduced himself. 'Schmitt,' she said, in response. 'Frau Schmitt.' She was quite a bit older than Annelie, with short, tightly curled grey hair. Alongside Annelie, she seemed rather plain. She returned his smile demurely, wiping her hands on her apron.

'I'm glad you're here, Frau Schmitt,' said Annelie, entering the house. 'Philipp's come to have a look at Baboo. He's going to find out who did such a terrible thing to her.' She glanced around for any sign of the cat. 'Where is she? Have you seen her?'

'She's in 'er basket,' Frau Schmitt replied, in a broad local burr. 'Asleep at last, bless 'er.'

Annelie led Philipp up a spiral staircase and there, on a wide windowsill, lay a tabby cat in a soft basket placed in a sunny spot. She was fast asleep, her flank gently rising and falling with every breath. Annelie looked at her tenderly for a moment. 'Ah well, let's leave her for a bit. She needs her sleep, after what she's been through. Do you have time for a cup of coffee, perhaps?'

'All the time in the world,' said Philipp, smiling.

It was true, he had no particular claims on his time. In

fact, he arranged everything in his life to avoid being plagued by regular employment. He was master of his daily routine – although perhaps 'routine' wasn't the right word for it. Every day, Philipp juggled three or even four different jobs, and it didn't faze him. On the contrary, he enjoyed being on the move, keeping things fresh. He knew nearly everyone in Hofheim, and they knew him: there probably wasn't a single person in the town who hadn't encountered him in at least one of his many occupations. If he hadn't sold you insurance, or licensed your car, he'd probably moved house for you, or done the catering for some family occasion. His removals company was in constant demand, even if his lorry and van were often to be seen taking a break on the roadside, smoke pouring out from under their bonnets (they had complicated inner lives, he was the first to admit). He employed a motley crew of 'boys' to help with packing, carrying, and driving – some of them a little too long in the tooth now to do much besides making the tea. His youngest son had come on board, and helped him run the business, and he was proud that it was a family affair. With all these commitments, he still found time to drive to Berlin or London from time to time, to see his grandchildren. There were parties to go to as well, of course, most evenings.

On those evenings when there was no party marked in his calendar, he would sit in his basement office and work long into the night, his desktop hidden beneath tottering stacks of paper, post-it notes, dirty plates and the occasional discarded yoghurt pot. The mindless babble from the TV masked the noises from the darkened house around him, the creaking of the stairs, the gurgling in the pipes. On evenings like this, he secretly wished he had someone to sit next to him on the sofa and watch TV with him, someone to cook and eat with, to talk with. Someone with whom he could just stop and do nothing at all, and for that to be okay.

That was why he had no objections to a coffee. None whatsoever. Annelie gave instructions to Frau Schmitt, and the old woman hurried obligingly out of the room. 'She's a sweetie, she really is,' said Annelie wistfully, ushering Philipp over to a light blue couch in the corner. The whole house was remarkably clean, Philipp noticed. Or perhaps it was just that he'd got used to the squalor and clutter of his own household. It was possible that all normal people lived like this, with couches laden with colourful cushions, and glass coffee tables bearing newspapers and magazines, all artfully displayed. Annelie kicked off her sandals and pulled her bare legs up onto the sofa. Her toenails, Philipp couldn't help noticing, were painted a livid green. He settled himself next to her, nearly drowning in the softness of all the upholstery.

While they were waiting for their coffee, Annelie explained how she'd come to live in Hofheim. A former boyfriend of hers had lived here, and she'd followed him down from Hamburg, where she was originally from. She'd fallen for the little town, nestled in the hills, with its proud onion-domed church towering over its half-timbered houses, and when the boyfriend had moved away, she'd decided to stay. She visited her parents in Hamburg from time to time, and worked in nearby Frankfurt as a graphic designer, commuting by train. She loved her new life. And Hofheim was a wonderful place to call home. She was happy, she said. At least, she had been, until all of this.

She asked Philipp about his life, and he found himself baring his soul to her, telling her about his mother, how she'd been born in a Bavarian castle, how she'd met his father in Lich after the war, though he was from Berlin. They'd looked for somewhere to start a family, and found no better place for it than Hofheim, especially since it was close to Frankfurt, where his father worked for a photographic company, and had to travel around the world attending fairs and exhibitions. Philipp's uncle, who was an architect, had built their family house in Marxheim, where he grew up. The upper story of the house was given over to Philipp and his four siblings, and contained two bathrooms, a toilet, five bedrooms and even a darkroom for developing photos, and the children were generally left to their own devices. It was an idyllic childhood, and when his siblings moved away from the town, Philipp had decided to stay and look after his mother and bring up his own children in the family home. He explained to Annelie that he'd become a father at an early age, just nineteen: early enough that he'd had to take his small daughter with him when he went to collect his exam results from school. The mother of his child was finishing her apprenticeship as a carpenter at the time, and since he'd had to repeat his final year, he'd ended up taking their baby to school with him. Having a small child with you in class had some benefits: if he didn't know the answer to a question, he'd simply give her leg a gentle pinch, and she'd yelp, and then the teacher would let the two of them leave the classroom until the baby had calmed down again. He was widely praised for being such a good and committed father. They'd made a great team, he and his daughter!

Annelie laughed at this, and the two of them were deep in conversation when Frau Schmitt reversed into the room with a tray of refreshments, which she unloaded onto the coffee table: cups of hot cappuccino, full to the brim, with milk foam sprinkled with dark chocolate powder; a ceramic bowl with sugar; two spoons; a jug of milk; and a plateful of almond biscuits. Ordinarily, Philipp would have dived at the biscuits: he had a sweet tooth, and anything that tasted even vaguely of marzipan was like catnip to him. But they barely even registered with him, occupied as he was with Annelie's company and the chemistry that he felt sure was developing between them. As the caffeine coursed through his veins, he felt a restoration of some vital life force. It was rare, he realised, that he spoke about his childhood, or anything else much beyond the small print on an insurance policy, or the expiry date on a vehicle licence. Most people he spoke with knew everything about him already, so there was no need for explanations. And on the rare occasion that he met anyone new, they generally seemed to prefer the conversational shallows. With Annelie, he didn't quite know what was happening. There was just something about her that made him trust her, and he felt safe opening up to her, confiding in her. The fact that she was undeniably very attractive was no longer the most important thing about her. Instead, it was the way she was at ease with herself that captivated him, her laughter – earthy and surprisingly deep – and the kindness in her eyes.

For her part, Annelie felt more and more comfortable herself. At first glance, the man in the scruffy T-shirt, his arms all smeared with engine oil, had been a disappointment. She'd expected someone suave, debonair, befitting the role of a sophisticated sleuth. Someone with a bit of class, who'd immediately be able to see through any shady character. Admittedly, she didn't know much about all that – only what she'd seen in one or two old movies. Her first impression of Philipp had been that he was a bit of a shady character himself. But the more time she spent with him, the more layers he seemed to have. It was rare to be able to speak with a man about such personal things, and it felt like they'd really hit it off. She also liked the dimple that appeared in his cheek whenever he smiled.

It was Annelie's laughter that eventually woke Baboo. She stretched one leg out in front of her with splayed claws, and yawned so deeply that from where they were sitting on the sofa they could see the pink roof of her mouth. Annelie jumped up, grabbed Philipp's hand, and pulled him over to where the cat lay on the windowsill. She gently stroked Baboo's head, and the cat closed her eyes and purred. Then she carefully lifted one forepaw out from under the cat's body and showed it to Philipp. He could see clearly where the paw had been severed. The wound had been cleanly stitched, and seemed to have healed quite well. All the same, Baboo didn't take kindly to having her stump dragged out for a stranger to see: she jumped down from her bed rather gingerly, and hobbled on three legs towards the kitchen.

'Poor Baboo,' Annelie sighed. 'I really can't think how it happened.'

Philipp furrowed his brows. 'I'd say that whoever did this has experience with amputations. I worked in a hospital for a while, so I've seen a good deal of surgery. To make it look as good as that, you've got to know what you're doing.' Actually, the sight of blood invariably made Philipp pass out, an unfortunate habit that had led to him being banned from the operating theatre after he'd had to be wheeled out on the trolley in place of the patient. So his insight into how operations worked was, in truth, rather limited.

But Annelie didn't know that. 'Yes!' she exclaimed, somewhat breathlessly. 'That's exactly what I thought. It all looks a bit too neat, doesn't it? I mean, they've taken a great deal of care about it. How strange. Who would do a thing like that?'

'Can I ask you a personal question?' he ventured.

Annelie looked surprised. 'How personal?'

'Do you have any particular enemies?'

'Enemies? I don't know. What kind of enemies?'

'Well, someone you might have had a fight with. A disagreement. A neighbour, for example… or your ex-boyfriend?'

She laughed out loud. 'No! No, not him! He loved Baboo

as much as I do. And he's the most ham-fisted person I know. He couldn't darn a sock, let alone stitch up a paw!'

Philipp, who'd been looking out of the window, breathed a sigh of relief. There was, he thought, just a chance that this might work out.

'In that case, I'd better make some enquiries. See if the neighbours have noticed anything suspicious. That's always a good place to start. And I have a friend who's a surgeon, I'd like to get his opinion. Yes, I think we should make a start right away.'

Annelie gave a little squawk and threw her arms around him. 'Does this mean… you'll take the case?'

'Yes. Yes, of course,' he said. 'I mean, I'll do what I can. No promises.'

As Annelie planted a kiss on his cheek, Philipp noticed Frau Schmitt at the door. Clearly embarrassed by the sudden display of unwarranted affection, she beat a hasty and soundless retreat, before the kiss was even completed.

'Thank you!' Annelie beamed. 'I'm so grateful. You don't know how much this means to me.'

THREE
A promising start

Accompanying Philipp out to his car, Annelie scratched Maschka's head one more time and gave Philipp another hug. Then he started the engine, and the calm tranquillity of the afternoon was shattered.

As he pulled out of the courtyard, Philipp saw out of the corner of his eye the net curtains twitch slightly in one of the windows. Annelie was standing in front of the house, the sun casting a halo around her golden head, waving at him. And then he turned the corner, and she was gone.

'Well, Maschka,' he said. 'Who'd have thought it?'

Maschka had taken up her customary place on the passenger seat, her tongue flapping in the wind. The two of them made their way down the hill, the car roaring away contentedly.

At home, Philipp was immediately sucked back into the flow of his day. He'd barely opened the front door when the phone started ringing. Good smells wafted through from the kitchen where his housemate Michi was making lunch. Philipp clamped the phone between his shoulder and ear, and clip-clopped down the stairs into his cellar office. The customer on the line was keen to come in for a chat about his liability insurance, and Philipp gave him an appointment, which he marked on his wall calendar. 'I'm going to need more biscuits,' was his immediate thought.

Lunch was *Königsberger Klopse*, a popular German dish consisting of meatballs in cream sauce, and this was interrupted by three more phone calls. When they'd finished eating, he and Michi carried their plates into the kitchen and stacked them in the broken dishwasher. Philipp was waiting for an unwanted dishwasher to become available through his removals company – it was all just a matter of time. Meanwhile, a wooden spoon had been rammed into its hinges to stop anyone actually using it – a necessary precaution to avoid the kitchen being flooded again.

After lunch, he drove his tractor out to his fields at the edge of town to bring in the hay, and then took Schimmi out for a short ride, to give the horse his daily exercise. This was followed by a meeting with a client whose fully comprehensive insurance wasn't as comprehensive as she would like. Then there was a quick stop at the bank to extend the mortgage on his barn, and one or two other commitments that had to be kept. When all this had been ticked off his to-do list, he embarked on some food shopping, because he had guests coming for dinner: pretzel soup, an intriguing yet tasty starter; roast beef with rosemary potatoes and fennel and some good gravy; and then a cinnamon sorbet with poached plums. And he needed biscuits too, of course, for his insurance clients.

It was a busy day, but even so he found that, at unexpected moments, memories of his morning with Annelie kept popping into his head. When the tractor's clutch got stuck on the way back from the fields, a vision of her green toenails shot into his mind. While urging Schimmi into a gallop across the fields, he suddenly recalled Annelie scratching Maschka's head. And while pushing a shopping trolley around Aldi, he was brought up short by the vivid recollection of her goodbye kiss.

Tsk tsk tsk. He shouldn't let his thoughts wander like this. She was out of his league. But the slight frisson of possibility gave him the pleasant feeling of being young again, even if it was nothing more than building castles in the air.

The evening flew by in a blur of delicious food, laughter, and wine, with the lit candles casting a warm, flickering glow over the familiar faces of his guests. They all seemed to be thoroughly enjoying themselves. The only person who wasn't fully present was Philipp himself. At the back of his mind, like a persistent daydream, floated Annelie and the mysterious case of the cat with the missing paw. It was now his responsibility. He resolved to send her a text message later, even though he had nothing to update her about. He could at least thank her for the coffee. Manners and all that.

When the last dinner-party stragglers had left, Philipp found he was much too tired to do any clearing up. He left the dirty plates and glasses where they were on the dining table, blew out the candles and headed for bed. Maschka was already asleep in the corridor, her tail twitching excitedly, pedalling her legs. 'Good night, Maschka,' he said. 'Sweet dreams.' He heaved himself up the creaking wooden staircase. Slumping onto the bed, he kicked off his clogs and let his jeans fall in a crumpled heap on the floor. Then he grabbed his mobile and tapped out a short message: 'Thanks for the coffee. Will be in touch as soon as I've found out anything. Sleep well.' He quickly pressed 'Send' before any second thoughts could present themselves, then snuggled up under the duvet. Soon the soporific burbling from the TV had lulled him to sleep.

The smell of fresh coffee and sizzling bacon drifted lazily through the open window and tickled his nose. Drowsily opening his eyes, Philipp saw that the sky was blue, and the sun was shining. He stretched and yawned – he hadn't slept as well as that for a long time. What a feeling! He glanced at his mobile. Nothing. But it was still early. Outside, on the terrace, Michi was tucking into a hearty fried breakfast. Just what he needed at the start of a new case.

As soon as he got into his basement office, Philipp picked up the phone and called Christoph, his surgeon friend.

'How are you, Philipp, old buddy?' came the familiar voice down the line. 'What do I owe this pleasure to?'

'I've got something to run by you, Christoph. Have you got a minute?'

'For you, all the time in the world. I'm due in surgery in five minutes though, so shoot!'

'Right. Well, it's about an amputation.'

There was an uncomfortable silence at the other end of the line, so Philipp pressed on: 'If I wanted to amputate a limb, I'd need to get a surgeon to do it, right?'

'You certainly would,' came the reply at once. Philipp detected a note of anxiety in Christoph's voice.

'But what if it was an animal? Could anyone do that, in theory? Someone without any expertise?'

'Oh, Philipp, is it your poor horse? I can come over later if you need. Don't even think of doing it yourself.'

Philipp laughed at his friend's earnestness. 'No, no, I'm asking on behalf of a friend. You see, she has a cat, and someone's hacked off one of its paws, and it looks like a professional job. It's been sewed up very nicely. The cat's not happy about it, of course, but it seems like it's going to live. What I'd like to know is, could that have been done by anyone – let's say, someone who's handy with a needle and thread? Or would it require medical training?'

Christoph sounded mightily relieved. 'Sounds to me like they had some experience, at least. There'd have been plenty of blood. They'd have had to apply pressure to the wound until the bleeding stopped, possibly used a torniquet. Then, as you say, they'd have needed to know how to do the stitches – you can't just use any old bit of cotton, it'd never hold. And needless to say, none of this is easy to do, let alone with an animal that's in pain and won't sit still.'

'Presumably there are ways of putting a cat to sleep before you have a chop at it?'

'Sure, that's not so hard. Though if you get the dose wrong, it might never wake up.'

'So you're saying it's possible, at least? If you did your homework?' Philipp picked up a pencil and started doodling on a pad on his cluttered desktop.

'Are you sure this cat wasn't just injured in a fight? Maybe it got its paw squashed in a door or something? Your car door, for instance – it wouldn't be the first time that's caused an injury.'

Philipp laughed momentarily. 'That's what I thought at first, a fight or something. But then I had a look at the cat myself. That stump, it's as pretty as you like. Textbook. If I needed my own leg amputating, I'd want this guy to do it.'

'Pretty strange thing to do to somebody's cat,' mused Christoph. 'Especially if the paw was healthy before it was done.'

'Seems like it was in full working order.'

'Some people are just sick in the head, my friend.'

They both fell silent.

Christoph broke the silence. 'Sorry, Philipp, I'm being beeped. They need me in surgery right now. Good luck with the case.'

'Thanks, Christoph. Feels like I'm going to need it.'

The line went dead. For a moment longer Philipp went on doodling, lost in a reverie that may have had something to do with memories of his time working in the hospital: the hustle and bustle, the nurses in their uniforms, the atmosphere of rigorous calm and efficiency all around him. Ah, the golden days of youth, how fast they slip away…

He looked down at his doodle. It resembled something a psychiatric patient might come up with after a month in solitary confinement. And what he'd thought was a pad of paper was in fact a letter to an insurance client, awaiting despatch. Oh well, no time to retype it now – they could have the doodle, free of charge.

If he was going to hack off a cat's paw, he thought, for the sake of argument, where would he do it? Not out in the street, that's for sure. It wouldn't be quick, and you'd need to keep the cat contained, at least until any tranquiliser took effect. Besides, there was the likelihood of being seen. It just wouldn't be practical, either. You'd need somewhere clean, even sterile. You'd need all your equipment to hand. And the mess would have to be cleaned up afterwards too. No, it just wasn't something you'd risk doing outdoors.

If it had happened indoors, though, the chances of there being any witnesses were very slim. It was hard to know where to start asking questions. Still, he could always begin with the neighbours. Wasn't that what real detectives did? And besides, it would give him an excuse to look in on Annelie. He didn't want to send her another text so soon, especially as he hadn't heard back since his previous one; but if he was in the area anyway, it would perhaps seem natural for him to drop by, just to let her know he was working on the case. And if he had something to report, so much the better.

He suddenly had another thought. Hadn't he seen that there was a meadow for rent in Langenhain, just near

Annelie's? He'd noticed it because he'd been thinking recently that Schimmi could do with somewhere to graze in the company of other horses – he was getting on now, was already more than forty years old, and was no longer the wild stallion he'd been in his youth, when he'd needed to go on journeys of self-discovery up the *autobahn*. He'd calmed down a lot, and was settling admirably into middle age, a development that Philipp attributed to his own careful nurturing: all the love and affection he'd lavished on that horse, the daily exercise, the lengthy massages he'd given him, and the dedication with which he'd pulled so frequently on his tail, putting his entire bodyweight into the task, something he was convinced was good for the horse, and the key to his longevity. But some of the neighbours had complained about the piles of dung and the constant neighing, so maybe having him in the garden was no longer sustainable. It had only meant to be a temporary solution anyway. If the meadow was suitable, he'd have every reason to pop over to Langenhain every day, to exercise his horse and keep an eye on things.

Philipp felt renewed purpose and energy coursing through his veins. There were things to do, a crime to solve! He grabbed an old black felt hat that was lying on a pile of papers. It had been his dad's, and it would suit him very well while he was out investigating – it looked the part, rather dashing in its old-fashioned chic, and it would no doubt give him a certain edge. There was no time to change out of the T-shirt he was wearing, but no matter, it was too warm for a shirt and jacket anyway. His clogs clattered up the staircase, and he clicked his tongue for Maschka, who immediately rushed to his side. They swept out of the house in perfect synchrony, a little like the A-Team on the TV, and jumped into one of Philipp's cars – this time a turquoise Opel with red leather seats. The engine started up almost at once, and they drove off at considerable speed, if at slightly lower volume than in the MG.

FOUR
A witness with something to hide

The car came to a juddering halt outside Annelie's house, and Philipp leapt out, pulling the brim of the black felt hat down as he made a beeline to the door. He rang the doorbell in joyful anticipation of more almond biscuits, coffee, and company.

He waited. There was no sign of life behind the door. He pressed the doorbell again. Nothing. Not a sound from inside. He looked at his watch: half past ten in the morning. Maybe she was at work? Just to make sure, he rang the bell one last time, holding it down for a few extra seconds. Still nothing.

He made his way back to the car, opened the door and sat down heavily behind the steering wheel. Maschka looked back at him with a furrowed brow. He stroked her head, relieved that he didn't have to try and mask his sense of disappointment. Maschka, at least, was always on his side. She seemed to understand him. With her, he could be fully himself.

For some reason, he no longer felt quite so confident about pursuing this investigation. His chances of success now appeared vanishingly remote. It all seemed like drudgery, a dreadful chore. He'd been kidding himself all along. He looked at himself in the rear-view mirror. The hat, in particular, seemed a ridiculous affectation. What if it got him laughed at? He took it off, turned it round and round in his hands, and then placed it decisively on the hat shelf behind him.

Best just to make a start, he told himself. Knock on one of the neighbours' doors and ask if they'd seen anything suspicious. Even if they hadn't, he'd still have something to tell Annelie, whenever she returned.

The house to the left of Annelie's was surrounded by a hedge that had been trimmed with almost obsessive precision. Two narrow flower-beds flanked the path to the front door. The sound of Philipp's clogs echoed between the high walls of the courtyard. There was a bronze door knocker in the shape of a dachshund, and Philipp lifted it by the tail and let its hind legs swing back heavily against the metal plate. The noise it made was startlingly loud, but it only intensified the deathly quiet inside the house. He waited a moment, and then struck with the hind legs once again. This time it produced a shuffling from within.

The door opened, but only a hand's width. A thick metal chain prevented it from opening further. From a position of safety beyond the chain, a woman peered out at him. She seemed to be in her late sixties, though Philipp couldn't be sure – her face was caked in thick, lurid make-up, like a pastiche of a Hollywood starlet. A stench of sickly perfume slapped him across the face. She glared at him from beneath heavily mascaraed eyelashes.

'What do you want? We're not buying anything.'

'Good morning, Madam,' Philipp began, in what he hoped was a disarmingly friendly sort of way. 'My name is Philipp.'

'So?'

'So... I have a few questions for you if you don't mind. Can I come in?'

She gave him a look as if he were some foul-smelling substance on the sole of her shoe. 'No you cannot. I don't even know who you are. Jehovah's Witness? Travelling salesman? I really don't have any time for this.'

'No, no, not at all. I'm a private investigator. You know, a detective. It's about your neighbour.'

The woman's face lit up suddenly, as if a lamp had been switched on behind the colourful shade of her painted skin. 'Oh, about *her*. In that case... do come in.'

Instantly she began fumbling with the chain, and threw the door wide open to let him in. 'It was only a matter of time before she went too far. Please, come this way.'

Philipp followed her down the narrow, unlit corridor, into the shadowy depths of the house. She moved surprisingly quickly, and for a moment he lost sight of her in the gloom, only for the painted head to reappear out of a doorway further down.

'This way,' she said, batting her extraordinary eyelids.

Philipp looked around the living room with apprehension. It stood in stark contrast to Annelie's, in which he'd spent the previous morning. Where that had been spacious, brightly furnished and filled with light, this was sepulchral and overcrowded, with the barest hint of daylight penetrating the protective ranks of pine trees that stood just beyond the windows. The room was cluttered with dark oak furniture, and a gaggle of black leather sofas huddled around an orange-tiled coffee table like witches around a cauldron. On the window ledges stood a coven of porcelain figures, while several enormous dolls in ruched dresses and white aprons sat stiffly on a high shelf, staring down at him with sad, painted eyes.

The woman threw herself down on one of the leather

sofas and, with a tilt of her head, invited Philipp to join her.

As he sat down gingerly on the edge of the sofa, Philipp thought of Maschka, lying faithfully on the red leather seat of the car outside, in the sunshine, imagining her sticking her head out of the open window waiting for his return and wondered how he'd gone so quickly from that world into this.

'So, what has she done now, then?' The woman looked at him eagerly, reaching for his hand. 'Tell me all about it.'

From this distance, Philipp could see the pores in the woman's face, even through the thick plaster-coating of make-up. There was a thin layer of sweat on her brows, and the roots of her dark hair were ashen grey. His throat felt dry, but he decided not to ask for a drink – best to get this over with as quickly as possible.

'Well, Frau…' he hesitated, and she jumped in obligingly with 'Frau Kaaserer. Elke Kaaserer.'

'Elke. Very good. And I'm Philipp.'

At this, she put her fingertips to her lips and giggled like a schoolgirl – whether in amusement at his first name (though he'd already mentioned that at the door) or in embarrassment at his use of hers, Philipp couldn't tell. He backed away from her a little, and, freeing his hand from her grasp, reached for his notebook in the back pocket of his jeans.

'Can I ask, Elke – how long have you known Annelie?'

'Annelie…?' Frau Kaaserer's face took on a bovine expression.

'Your next-door neighbour,' he said, trying to keep the exasperation out of his voice. 'Frau Janssen.'

'Oh, is that her name? Janssen. Strange. Not from round here.'

Clearly, Frau Kaaserer was less well informed than she liked to suggest. Or at least, she was better at twitching curtains than properly getting to know her neighbours.

'It's been three or four years, maybe,' she went on. 'I couldn't say exactly when she moved in. But some things you can't help noticing, can you?'

'Such as?'

'Well, she has a lot of… visitors. Male ones, if you know what I mean.'

'Tradesmen, would you say, or…'

'Gentlemen callers,' she interrupted, eyes glowing like hot coals. 'Different ones all the time. Well, she's obviously not from round here. It's a different lifestyle in the big cities, isn't it? But here, these things don't go unnoticed.' She reached for his hand once again, and Philipp flinched. 'Rather loose, I'd say, wouldn't you?'

Philipp said nothing but, drawing his hand away from hers, pretended to make notes in his notebook.

Frau Kaaserer seemed to need no further encouragement, and went on: 'Sometimes there are parties, of course. Well, it's not right. Where does she think she is? This is a nice quiet respectable place. All that noise, it's anti-social. She even has loud music playing when she's there on her own. Imagine!'

She seemed to be looking for a reaction from him, but he kept his head down, taking notes, and soon she continued: 'And the drinking! Doesn't she know the recycling bags are see-through? She's absolutely shameless! There are children living around here, and what are they going to make of it? That's no way to behave. And she has no children of her own, it's patently obvious. Well, she probably waited too long. No one to blame but herself. These young girls, they think they have all the time in the world, and then pfff, the chance is gone. Do you have any children? I bet you do.'

Philipp looked up, startled by the sudden change of tack. 'Yes,' he said. 'Four.'

Elke clapped her hands together in delight: 'Oh, how

wonderful! My goodness. Four! They must keep you busy. Ah, but it's different for a father, of course. With my Fritzl, I had my work cut out for me. He's moved out now. He has his own place, just three doors down. We bought the land for him, and he built the house. Had it built, of course! Ah well, but it does feel empty when they move out. And once they're gone, they're gone, they don't come back, do they? Apart from the Sunday roast, he always comes back for that.' She leant closer to him and whispered conspiratorially: 'His wife's no good at it. No good at all. Fritzl is very particular about his Sunday roast. He knows what he likes, my Fritzl.'

Philipp was hardly listening now. He was thinking about his own children. As dearly as he loved them, he was perfectly happy that they were living in three different countries, and not three doors down the road. Their mothers had always had full working lives, and he'd enjoyed life as a hands-on dad. When they'd been little, he'd played endless board games with them on the floor in the living room, having long tournaments of chess and backgammon, with prizes for the winners. He'd taken them along to work meetings with clients, got them to help out in the restaurant kitchen, and even carry boxes on removals jobs. It did them good to be exposed to the real world. He'd even appeared on a TV show once, when the children were all young, and as a result he'd achieved a certain level of fame as a single father looking after three children (the fourth hadn't yet appeared). He'd been described in an on-screen caption as a 'super father with three kids', and it had become a bit of a nickname for a while. He wasn't much into Sunday roasts – his speciality was an outstanding avocado soup with sherry, and if it had to be a roast, he could do a roast beef that would make an Englishman turn green with envy.

But he'd better pull himself together. This wasn't about a competition in parenting, it was about a crime.

'Do you know anything about Baboo?' he said, interrupting whatever it was she was babbling about.

She stopped short and looked at him as if he were from a different planet.

'Your neighbour's cat,' he went on. 'Baboo.'

This only seemed to confuse her further. 'A cat? I thought you wanted to know about that ghastly woman.'

'No, it's about her cat.'

Frau Kaaserer looked crestfallen. Philipp almost enjoyed her disappointment. 'You might have seen it about,' he said. 'A tabby cat. Rather pretty.'

'Yes, well, I've seen a cat. I've no idea if it belongs to her.'

It was as if a dark cloud had cast a shadow over her. The lights had gone out in her smouldering eyes, and they were nothing but ash. Perhaps she'd been hoping that something dreadful had happened to this annoying neighbour of hers, but now that she knew it concerned the cat, she'd simply lost interest.

But then another thought struck him: perhaps she was on the defensive now. Was it possible that she'd been so outraged by Annelie's lifestyle – the loud music and parties, the 'gentlemen callers' – that she'd taken matters into her own hands? He could imagine that here was a woman who, rather than confronting her neighbour directly, would employ more devious ways to issue a warning. In that case, he would have to be devious himself.

'You must be a terrific cook, Frau Kaaserer... Elke.' He smiled sweetly at her. 'I mean, for your son and his family to come over every Sunday. Family is so important, I think, don't you? And it's things like this that keep families together.'

A little colour had come back into Frau Kaaserer's face. 'He does love my roast pork, does Fritzl.'

'Who doesn't love a good roast pork! A fine German

tradition.' He grimaced inwardly at his own shamelessness. 'And I bet yours is second to none.'

'It's not easy to get it right,' she said, reaching again for his hand. 'It can go dry and tasteless if you're not careful.'

'But yours, Elke, is nice and succulent, I imagine.' He left his hand there for as long as he could bear it. 'And I dare say you carve it yourself?'

'Who else? Of course I do the carving. Fritzl says it's a man's job, but I insist. I have an electric carving knife that goes through it like butter.'

'Ah, then you make short work of it! I've always wanted an electric carving knife. It must be useful for all sorts of jobs. I wonder, where do you buy such a thing?'

'I have no idea,' she replied. 'It was my husband who bought it, God bless him. He passed away years ago. Heart attack.' She dabbed at her eyes with a tissue which she'd produced from some fold of her sleeve.

'I am sorry to hear that, Frau Kaaserer.' Philipp did indeed now feel a touch sorry for the woman, and a little guilty that he hadn't paid proper attention to her as she'd prattled on. Clearly, she was desperately lonely.

'It's not easy, being on your own,' she said, snivelling a little. 'Still, I have Fritzl. He's a great comfort. And who knows, maybe there will be grandchildren soon.'

'Grandchildren are always a blessing,' he said. 'I have six, and all of them are wonderful.'

'Six! Good gracious. And you're still such a youngster.'

'Well, I had children early. And no regrets about that.' She gave his hand a firm squeeze.

'Now,' he said, seeing his chance, 'About that cat…'

But at that instant, Frau Kaaserer propelled herself up from the sofa, exclaiming: 'Goodness me, is that the time?' Looking around, Philipp could see no clock. He knew then that he was defeated.

After the gloom of Frau Kaaserer's living room, the bright sunlight outside nearly blinded him as he made his way back to the car. He stood for a moment, his hand on the car door, blinking, trying to dispel the image he had in his mind's eye of a painted old hag wielding an enormous carving knife over a terrified tabby that was tied to an orange-tiled coffee table. And then his vision returned and he could see Maschka sticking her muzzle out of the car window, whimpering in joyful anticipation, waiting faithfully for him.

As soon as he opened the door, she jumped out, and they went to look for a tree. Maschka, being female, didn't need trees to wee against, but simply crouched down; on the other hand, Philipp did, and he hadn't had the courage to ask Frau Kaaserer if he could use her bathroom – she'd wanted him out of the house, and the feeling was mutual. Still, he'd learned something valuable. Frau Kaaserer was handy with a carving knife. He'd be keeping a keen eye on her, that much was certain.

Once they'd both relieved themselves, it was time for a quick recce around the outside of Annelie's house. Philipp tried to conduct a search of the courtyard as unobtrusively as possible, knowing there was a good chance he was being watched from an upstairs window. Frau Kaaserer, he felt sure, would equally be keeping an eye on him, and he didn't want to give the game away, any more than could be helped.

He wasn't sure what he was looking for, exactly. Signs of a struggle, perhaps. Blood stains. Grass that had been trampled on. Tufts of fur left on a fence. In short, anything that pointed towards Baboo's paw having been severed outside, either by force or by accident. It would overturn his conviction that it must have happened indoors, but a good detective tests every assumption.

He found nothing at all out of the ordinary. Only the bins, standing in a neat row, clearly labelled, the courtyard swept clean, the trees swaying gently in the breeze. No sign of a struggle or bloodshed anywhere.

It had been more than an hour since he'd rung Annelie's doorbell, and it struck him that she might have returned home while he'd been at Frau Kaaserer's. Besides, he'd made some progress – however small – and was eager to report it to her. So, with renewed hope, he rang the doorbell again. And once again, there was no response to it.

He pulled out his mobile and sent Annelie a quick message: 'Just questioned the first witness. I have some information for you. When would be good for a catch-up?' Even if she was at work and her phone was turned off, it was nearly lunchtime, and she'd surely check her messages then.

He began to think about lunch himself. He could stop off at the shops for something to take home, but then he thought about the piles of dirty plates in every room of the house, and began to feel less enthusiastic about the idea. There was a good doner kebab place in the Zeilsheimer Road, pretty much on his way home. It would save a lot of time, and time was money, wasn't it? Not only that, it was also a critical factor when you were in the middle of an investigation. There was no time to lose, or the trail might go cold. A doner kebab it would have to be, then.

At the kebab place, Maschka had to wait outside, so Philipp tied her lead to the metal bike stands, and she settled down to wait for him. As a mark of his gratitude, he arranged a water bowl for her, and gave her some dog treats, which were duly accepted. As he waited for his food, Philipp leant against the counter, drinking Fanta through a pink straw, and thought back over his encounter with Frau Kaaserer. Why did she have it in for Annelie? Was it mere jealousy – the way women of a certain age can be envious of a younger, more attractive woman? Or was there something else? His instinct told him that the woman simply had a problem with the old maxim 'live and let live'. There were plenty of people like her, who went round feeling spiteful towards others and harbouring grudges against them. But was this grudge deep enough to wish her neighbour actual harm? Was she so bitter and enraged that she would act on her impulse? And was she capable of doing something so cruel to an innocent animal? Philipp wasn't sure. He sensed only that there was something Frau Kaaserer was hiding, something that had led her to terminate his visit so abruptly. He'd need to investigate further.

He let his mind roam over some of the other things Frau Kaaserer had told him. How many men exactly had she seen coming and going at Annelie's house? Had Annelie hugged each of them, too, when they left, as she'd hugged him? He'd felt certain, at the time, that the hug she gave him had meant something significant – now he was no longer sure. Perhaps he was simply the latest in a long line of conquests.

When he left the kebab shop a few minutes later, he was feeling a little queasy. And it wasn't all down to the kebab.

FIVE

Love in the afternoon

Twice that afternoon his mobile phone buzzed in the pocket of his jeans, but on neither occasion was it a message from Annelie. Philipp sloped about the house like a lovesick teenager, and Maschka mooched around after him, like his surly shadow.

Why hadn't Annelie got back to him yet? Had she had second thoughts about offering him the case? Was she trying to put the brakes on it? Did she regret that kiss she'd given him when they were saying goodbye? Maybe there was another man, and she felt she had to give Philipp clear signals now that theirs could only ever be a business relationship? Well, if that was the situation, it was simply unreasonable of her not to respond to his messages: all he was trying to do was set up a meeting to discuss important matters with her relating to the case. This was no way to conduct an investigation – it was absurd!

Maschka looked up at him with what seemed like a worried expression. She always knew when something was upsetting him. 'Hey Maschka, my girl. Life isn't easy, take it from me.' The dog pressed her head against his thigh as if to reassure him. She knew life could be disappointing. 'How about a nice afternoon nap?' he said, and her tail lashed against the side of his leg.

With a careless swoop, Philipp toppled everything that was piled on the sofa onto the floor. Then he unfolded one of the large grey blankets that he always had lying around (the ones he used in his removals work) and cosied up under it with a paperback crime novel, his mobile phone close to hand. Soon he was fast asleep, with Maschka curled up on the floor next to him, her nose tucked under her tail. The house fell quiet around them.

Philipp felt safe and warm under his blanket, and when Annelie entered through the French windows, the room lit up and he felt a reassuring warmth flow through his whole body. Here she was, finally! He jumped up and smiled at her. As they embraced, he could feel the muscles in her back shifting underneath her thin jumper, and he inhaled the scent of her sun-warmed skin. 'How was work?' he asked, and she laughed. 'It was great. Come on, let's take a dip, it's so warm today.' She took his hand and led him outside, to the edge of a swimming pool. The water was blue and sparkled in the sunshine. Annelie was wearing a bright green bikini with white polka-dots contrasting brilliantly with all that blue as she dived headfirst into the water and then, surfacing, beckoned him to follow. 'The water's lovely!' she called to him. 'You ought to come in for a birthday swim, come on!' He followed her in, and it was true, the water was silky and warm, the perfect temperature. His body relaxed and he could feel his muscles stretch out sweetly as he swam length after length, going faster and faster as he scythed effortlessly through the water. Suddenly he found himself on the high diving board, far above the surface of the water, the one he'd always been scared to jump from, even as a child. But not today. No, today he could accomplish anything! He felt the springlike energy in the board beneath his feet as he took a run up and leapt from it in a death-defying *salto mortale*, entering the water perfectly, feet-first, without a splash. When he came up for air, his family and friends all cheered from the side of the pool. Annelie swam up to him, took him in her arms, and drew him towards her warm, sleek, welcoming body…

His mobile phone was ringing. Philipp threw off the blanket, started up from the sofa, and grabbed at it. 'Annelie?'

'Who's Annelie?' came an amused voice at the other end. His eldest daughter's voice. 'Have you got a new girlfriend?'

'Hello Schlumpa,' he sighed. Schlumpa was the childhood nickname he used for all his children, to avoid any kind of confusion. Being a Schlumpa marked you out as one of Philipp's children, that was all.

'Why haven't you told me about this "Annelie" yet?'

'Nothing to tell,' he said, shedding the last vestiges of his dream. The older his children got, the more impertinent they became. They seemed to feel entitled to know every last detail of his love life. He yawned, loudly.

'Did I wake you?'

'Doesn't matter. It's nice to hear from you.'

'I forgot about your afternoon nap,' she said in a tone that implied she'd known perfectly well he'd be kipping on the sofa.

'How are you, anyway?' he asked, fondly.

'I'm fine. The children are playing in the garden with the chickens, so I thought I'd grab five minutes with you, and ask you about your birthday. Any plans for it yet?'

'Not yet. Still looking for somewhere to have a bit of a party. Nowhere's quite big enough.'

'Why, how many are you inviting?'

'Oh, a couple of hundred maybe. I might ask Dieter if the Lido's free – it's certainly big enough, if he'll let us use the terrace and lawns. He might even close it to the public, and then we can all have a swim if we like.' The idea had just popped into his head from somewhere, and it seemed rather a good one.

'Sounds fun,' his daughter said, and at that same moment he heard in the background, down the line, the sound of an almighty crash. 'What's going on?' she shouted, presumably in the direction of her kids. They must have caused some kind of catastrophe in the garden, which Philipp knew was basically a building site, with a thousand different accidents waiting to happen. 'Sorry, dad, gotta go!'

'Give everyone my love!' he called, as the line went dead.

He sat for a while, staring at the grey blanket that had fallen in a heap on the floor. He didn't quite have the energy to get up off the sofa. His thoughts began circling back to Annelie again. Why hadn't she got in touch? Had he come on too strongly, perhaps? Had he got the wrong end of the stick? Women… they were an enigma to him. But an enigma he couldn't help trying to solve.

He managed to drag himself down to his cellar office, where there was a growing pile of paperwork demanding his attention. But it only bored him today. After half an hour sitting there, moving papers backwards and forwards and playing online chess against an unknown opponent, he pushed back his chair, exchanged his red leather clogs for his more serious black ones, and left the house, with Maschka like a shadow at his side.

A few minutes later he was standing at Annelie's door once again. As there were more neighbours still to investigate, he thought it was only sensible, since he was in the neighbourhood, to try her one more time.

He rang the doorbell and stepped back to wait. Straight away he noticed a scratch in the door frame at knee height. He bent down for a closer look. There was a fragment of something green lodged in the indentation in the wood. It looked like paint. He touched it with his fingertip, and it came off on his skin. He peered down at it. It was a curious shade of green.

Then without warning the front door swung open, and he fell forwards through the open doorway.

SIX

A little piece of the puzzle

Philipp found himself kneeling like a penitent on the sisal mat in Annelie's doorway, looking up at her cleaner. She seemed as surprised as he was, and let out a little yelp.

'Ah, Frau Schmitt,' he said, smiling up at her disarmingly, pleased he could remember her name. He got to his feet, using the door frame for support – then, recalling the fragment of green paint on his right index finger, put that hand quickly behind his back. 'I didn't think anyone was at home.'

Frau Schmitt wiped her hands on her apron. 'If it's 'er yer want, she's out at work.'

'Not to worry,' he said, trying not to let his disappointment show. Then, without really knowing why, he said: 'Actually, if it's not too much trouble, Frau Schmitt, I wonder if I might have a minute of your time?'

'Me?' she said, flushing slightly. 'Yer want to speak to me?'

'If you're not too busy.'

She seemed to hesitate for a moment. Philipp wondered if he'd overstepped the mark, but then she smiled, and said: 'Come in, if yer like.'

'Thank you.'

He followed her inside, carefully putting his right hand into the pocket of his jeans and wiping his fingertip on a bit of tissue he had in there. He ought to keep some resealable plastic evidence bags for this sort of thing, he realised, and made a mental note to buy some at the first opportunity.

'Would yer like some coffee, maybe?' she asked as she ushered him into the living room.

'If it's not too much bother, I'd love some,' he replied. It would give him a chance to spend longer in the house, he calculated, and Annelie was sure to return before long. In the meantime, he could have a bit of a chat with Frau Schmitt. She might even remember something useful. After all, she seemed to be around an awful lot. She might have seen something, or perhaps she could tell him a bit more about the neighbours. That dreadful Frau Kaaserer, for instance. Besides, he was rather hoping he might learn something more about Annelie. 'You'll have a coffee too, will you?' he asked.

'I was about to clean the bathroom,' she began, but then, as if making up her mind to give herself permission, added: 'But it's okay, I have a bit of time.'

'That's good,' he smiled.

While she was in the kitchen making the coffee, Philipp looked around the living room. Everything was exactly as he remembered it from the day before. The sun fell across the carpet and lit up the sofa with its plentiful cushions. An image of Annelie's naked feet shot through his mind, painfully, and he turned away and went to look at the spines of the books in the bookcase. He remembered someone saying you could get to know a person just by looking at what books they had on their shelves, but he'd got no further than *Doctor Zhivago* before the door opened and in came Frau Schmitt, backwards.

When she turned towards him, nudging the door shut with her bottom, Philipp could see that she was holding a tray piled high with treats. She must have guessed his predilection for sweet things from his previous visit.

'I don't believe it,' he said. 'Is that Niederegger Marzipan? How did you know? I can't resist it!'

'Help yerself,' she said, busying herself with the coffee.

He took one, carefully removed its red-and-gold wrapper, and popped it into his mouth, letting its inimitable flavours – intensely sweet and ever so slightly bitter – slowly unfold on his tongue. There was nothing quite like it!

Frau Schmitt had settled herself in an armchair with her cup of coffee, and was watching him closely. Feeling suddenly self-conscious, as if he'd been caught with his hand in the biscuit jar, he reached for the sugar tin and spooned three heaped teaspoons of sugar into his coffee.

'So,' he began, thinking it was time to get down to business, 'How long have you been working for Annelie?'

Frau Schmitt took a sip of her coffee and said: 'Nearly seven years now. Before this, I was selling pretzels. From one of those stalls at the train station in Frankfurt, yer know?'

Philipp nodded. He thought of the thick warm pretzels wrapped in paper, and the pleasant smell that wafted out from the little stalls on the station concourse. He could never walk past one without stopping to buy a pretzel for the train journey. They also did very nice filled bread rolls, and *Laugenstangen* covered in melted cheese, a favourite of his. His mouth was watering at the very thought of it.

Frau Schmitt, however, didn't seem to share his enthusiasm. 'It was an awful job, I hated every minute of it.'

'Oh. Why?'

'I was on my feet all day. Never a moment to sit down. Got fluid on my legs, I had to stop working there.' And she added, muttering, 'The soup was more expensive than the piece of bread yer put in it, if y'know what I mean.' Philipp didn't. It was some local Hessian expression, no doubt. He nodded.

'But I imagine it's better here, working for Annelie,' he said, wanting to get back to the matter in hand. If she'd been working here for seven years, she must know a good deal about her employer. 'She treats you well?'

'I can't complain.'

Philipp remembered how friendly Annelie been with her cleaner, and then he began to think about how friendly she'd been with *him*, and how the sun had made her hair shine when she'd been sitting there on the sofa right next to him. He sighed deeply.

Looking up, he saw Frau Schmitt watching him with a strange expression, somewhere between disgust and derision. He really must pull himself together – this was unprofessional behaviour.

'Annelie works in Frankfurt, I think?' he said, and Frau Schmitt nodded. 'May I ask, what hours do you work, here in the house?'

Frau Schmitt shrugged her shoulders. 'Well, it depends. I have a set of keys, so I let myself in when I need to. Sometimes, see, she doesn't come home in the evening, so there's nobody here to let me in. Other days she'll be home for lunch, or it's possible she'll be working from home all day. You never know with her, see.'

'I see. And how many days is it that you work, each week?'

'When we started it was Mondays and Thursdays. But sometimes I have to work overtime, especially if she's had one of her parties. See, the house can be in quite a state then, I tell you. I just stay until it's done. I have a key anyway, so sometimes I am here most days and do a few hours around other commitments, that's how it suits both of us best.'

Philipp wondered what it must be like to have a cleaner like Frau Schmitt – someone who just went on working until the job was finished. If she were his cleaner, she'd probably never go home.

Frau Schmitt presented him with the plate of marzipans again, and he helped himself, unwrapping another little parcel and popping it into his mouth.

'Delicious. Now, if you don't mind, Frau Schmitt, can you take me through the day of Baboo's injury? Do you remember anything unusual, anything out of the ordinary?' Then, remembering a detective show he'd once seen on TV, he added: 'It doesn't matter how small or insignificant it might seem to you, it may turn out to be useful.'

Frau Schmitt wrinkled her forehead in concentration and stared at the carpet for a while. He had a feeling she was trying to find the words for whatever was on her mind.

'You can tell me anything you like, Frau Schmitt. In complete confidence.'

She looked up then, right into his eyes... and said nothing.

'Really, anything at all, Frau Schmitt. There are no wrong answers here.'

She looked away again, and began twisting a handkerchief in her hands. Philipp waited as patiently as he could. There was definitely something she wanted to say – if only she'd just come out with it.

'Maybe... I have seen something,' she said, knotting the hankie in her lap. 'I'm not sure if it's important.'

'Any little thing, anything at all,' he said, trying to keep the irritation out of his voice. Frau Schmitt was still working away on the hankie, like she was knitting herself something for Christmas. 'You never know, it might be the little piece of the puzzle that solves the whole case.'

Frau Schmitt looked up at him with something like awe

in her expression. He knew it was now or never, and he reached out and placed a hand on hers. He left it there only for a moment, fighting a rising sense of repulsion at the dirty hankie that was now in contact with his hand. But it was enough. The momentary contact had wrought a change in her. Her features took on a liveliness that was almost striking, and as he looked at her again, he thought there might be an altogether different woman – a proud, appealing and really quite attractive one – hidden behind the drab carapace she wore for everyday purposes. She looked almost pretty.

She swallowed, and then began very slowly to speak. 'I went outside around eleven, to take the rubbish bags out. There was someone on the other side of the street, walking up and down. I thought maybe he was waiting fer someone. I'd never seen him before, that's why I remembered.'

'Excellent. And do you remember anything else about him? His age, perhaps? What he was wearing?'

Frau Schmitt went on twisting the hankie, so forcefully that her fingers had now gone perfectly white. 'He was about thirty, I'd say. And he was wearing a blue Adidas sports top and jeans.'

'What colour was his hair?'

'I don't know. He was wearing a cap, see. Like a baseball cap. I couldn't see his face.'

Damn, thought Philipp. Not much of a description. It could be almost anyone. If it came down to it, it would fit almost any of the younger men in his removals team. She'd practically described their uniform.

'Anything else you can remember? How long was he there? Which way did he go when he left?'

'I only saw him fer a minute. I had to get back to work.'

'And you didn't go on watching him after that?'

Frau Schmitt shook her head emphatically. 'Not paid to

look out the window, am I?'

'Quite right,' Philipp conceded, bitterly. He looked down at his own hands in his lap, where they were busy smoothing out the red-and-gold wrapper of the Niederegger Marzipan. Who was this mysterious man who'd been loitering outside the house on the very day Baboo was hurt? He wondered if the man was known to Annelie, and if perhaps he'd been rejected by her. It was certainly a possible motive. It was becoming ever more important that he spoke with Annelie directly. Where was she, and when would she return home? After the urgency she'd attached to the case, it was strange that she was now so cool and offhand about it. He scrunched the wrapper into a jagged little ball in his fist.

Frau Schmitt was looking at him without disguising her interest. Once again, he felt self-conscious under the glare of her gaze. 'So, have you any idea who did it?' she asked, with a disconcerting directness. Philipp was struck by how different she seemed now from the mild-mannered, self-effacing woman he'd taken her to be. He wondered if she'd changed, or if he'd been wrong about her all along. She was smiling at him now, and said: 'We're all just wondering who could have done something so awful to poor little Baboo.'

Philipp shuddered, inwardly. Was she taunting him? Of course not, she couldn't be. It was probably just his insecurity that made it seem that way.

'Rest assured, I will find out,' he said, hoping he sounded more authoritative. 'Thank you for your help, Frau Schmitt. I was hoping I might have the opportunity to speak to Annelie. Do you think she'll be back soon?'

Frau Schmitt shrugged again. 'She's probably staying the night with one of her boyfriends in Frankfurt. Who knows which one it'll be. She has a few, yer know.'

He caught the glint in her eye. It was time for him to

leave. 'Then I shall let you get back to your work, Frau Schmitt. You've been most helpful.'

Philipp left the house, reeling. He'd been wrong about Annelie, it was clear enough now. He was just a hired detective, someone she'd employed to do her dirty work. Now that she had him working on the case, she didn't have to concern herself with it any longer. She was free to do what she liked, see whomever she chose. She seemed to have a man in every port. He was nothing to her. How could he have thought she was interested in him? He was much too old for her. The kiss she'd given him was nothing more than a little sweetener for a lonely old man, something to keep him up late working on the job. She bought and sold people that way. He was just the same to her, really, as Frau Schmitt: nothing more, nothing less. They'd both been hired to do a job, and any kindness Annelie showed them was merely the currency she used to buy people's loyalty and service. Ah well, the scales had fallen from his eyes. He could see clearly now.

He got into his car and looked over at Maschka, who'd been waiting patiently for him. She seemed to know all about it.

'Let's go home, old girl,' he said.

As they drove the long and mournful way back, he reflected on his own chequered love-life. Why did he always seem to fall for the most unsuitable women? It was beyond his capacity to understand.

By the time he'd parked up outside his house, he'd reached a decision. He was no longer in this for the possibility of romance. That was behind him now. He was simply a professional, a private eye. And he'd do this job as well as he could. He'd find whoever had done that to Baboo, and he'd make them pay.

He even had a plan. There was a removals job booked

in for the next day. He could sound out the guys, use their connections to discover as much as he could about Annelie and this unknown man that Frau Schmitt had seen outside the house. That was the key to it all, he was convinced. Find out who that man was, and he'd have the case all sewn up.

Reaching into the pocket of his jeans for his house keys, he remembered the fragment of green paint he'd wrapped inside the bit of tissue. He took it out now and had another look at it. It really was very green.

SEVEN

Gut feeling

The bedside alarm went off at five in the morning. Philipp stumbled out of bed and got dressed without bothering to turn on the light.

He padded sleepily downstairs to the half-lit kitchen and made some strong coffee. He got out a packet of rye bread and popped two slices in the toaster, putting the rest of the packet on the table, together with a jar of Nutella, raspberry jam, peanut butter, marmalade, lemon curd, Danish chocolate sprinkles and butter. A good, solid breakfast. It was going to be a long day.

At a quarter past five, there was a knock at Philipp's door, and soon there were six men standing around his kitchen table, talking in hushed tones, holding hot mugs of tea and slices of bread, thickly spread with various toppings.

Ten minutes later, they were all inside Philipp's two removal vehicles, driving out of Hofheim towards the *autobahn*. Maschka had made a last-minute attempt to follow them out of the door, but Philipp told her that she had to look after the house while he was away and that Michi would feed her. The look in her eyes told him that she didn't feel that Michi's dog-sitting skills were up to the task, but a removals job really wasn't an outing for a dog: she would only get under everybody's feet. Lukas – the only one of the team besides Philipp who had a valid driver's licence – was driving the three-tonner, while Philipp himself was in the driving seat of the big six-tonne truck. In the front alongside him, Benjy and Holger had their feet up on the dashboard next to the heating vents, and they were still getting down the last of their breakfast toast. The radio was blaring out an eighties pop song.

'Hey, Philipp,' said Holger, just about awake enough now to start a conversation, 'When are you going to get yourself a vehicle that isn't a load of old junk?'

'What do you mean?' Philipp smiled, ruefully. 'This old girl? Listen to her. She's purring nicely.'

They listened for a moment. It was hard to hear the sound of the engine through the rattling that was coming from the chassis.

Holger snorted. 'Call that purring? This thing's going to fall apart any minute.'

'I can see the road down there,' said Benjy, peering down through a hole in the floor between his legs. 'Look, isn't that a white line?' The two of them started snickering.

'When you two put in a proper day's work, maybe I'll be able to afford a new truck.'

Philipp didn't mean to be so glum, but something had got his goat. Normally he'd play along with their jokes, laughing at their jibes, mostly at his own expense. They didn't have much of a work ethic, any of them. They'd never had it instilled in them. They liked to have a good time playing tricks on each other when they should be packing crates or stacking them into the back of the truck. The work was a bit of a drudge, and they didn't take much pride in it. Still, they always got it done, eventually. Sure, things got broken sometimes, especially if they'd been playing catch or joshing around. But mostly everything arrived at its destination in one piece. Philipp was the face of the business, so it was down to him to sort out any little mishaps, deal with customer relations. He also packed boxes and did more than his fair share of lugging around. He accepted it. After all, it was his business, he'd built it up from scratch, he ran it, it was all down to him. And he wasn't a bad boss. He was no tyrant. He could see the fun in things. Normally, he could.

Today, he just stared glumly through the windscreen at the rain glistening in the orange light of the streetlamps, and the smears left by the wipers on the glass. It was hard to be optimistic about anything much.

At around lunchtime they arrived at their destination, a small village about an hour outside Munich. They immediately got to work and were making good progress – the van was already half full – when Philipp's mobile rang. The screen displayed the caller ID: 'Annelie Home'. His mouth went dry, and his hand trembled a little. He jumped out of the van and went to find a quiet spot, tucked behind a hedge alongside the wall of the house. As he answered the call, he found that he could barely get out the words 'Good morning', his customary greeting, the one he invariably used, regardless of the time of day or night. 'Annelie?' he added, in a hoarse voice.

'Hello, yes, it's just me.' It was the cleaner's voice. He felt his excitement suddenly all drain away.

'Frau Schmitt! How nice.' He paused. There was a silence down the line. 'Is everything okay? Has something happened?'

He could hear her breathing, thick and throaty. 'Oh, well, I'm just a bit worried, y'know?'

You're not the only one, Philipp thought. He waited for her to continue.

'Fräulein Janssen didn't come home last night. Her bed

has not been slept in. I don't know what she wants me to do, she hasn't left a note. I'm not sure what I should do.'

Why was she telling him this? What did it have to do with him, what Annelie did with her time, who she spent the night with, whether or not she left instructions for her cleaner? He was starting to feel downright annoyed.

'I don't know how I can help, exactly, Frau Schmitt.'

'I've got such a bad feeling,' she said, her voice sounding tinny down the line. It was starting to grate on him. He felt he was going to snap at her if she didn't shut up. 'Can't you come over again, Philipp, please?' she said.

There was something raw and needy in her voice, and he felt a sudden sense of revulsion now at hearing her use his first name.

'It's not easy, right now. I'm in Munich. I can't just drop everything.'

She muttered a disappointed 'Oh', and he could hear her laboured breath again as she thought about it. 'In that case, I'm sorry I troubled you,' she droned.

Philipp was struck with a feeling of remorse. The poor woman, she was only concerned about what had happened to her employer. She had no one to turn to. He was the only person who might be able to help, and he was pushing her away.

'Wait,' he said. 'I'm back tomorrow. I could come round about three in the afternoon?'

'Yes, that would work fine,' came Frau Schmitt's voice. 'Tomorrow, about three. I will have some coffee ready.'

Philipp began to say that wouldn't be necessary, but she'd already hung up.

He put his phone in the breast pocket of his shirt, took off his glasses and rubbed the bridge of his nose between finger and thumb. This was getting serious. He was being drawn into something, he didn't quite know what – but he knew he was out of his depth. What he ought to do is call up his client and inform her that he couldn't continue the case. That would be the best course of action, for everyone involved. But he couldn't. She'd disappeared. He couldn't even do that.

And the thought of Annelie disappearing lay underneath it all, like a black rock. Where was she? What had happened to her? The old cleaner woman's words had set off a chain of images in his head that he could do nothing to stop: Annelie, staying on for drinks after work; music and lights, laughter, a hand on her arm, on her thigh, her hair lit up by disco lights. And then, it's too late for her to go home; he lives round the corner anyway, whoever he is; just there, on the Eschersheimer Landstrasse, or somewhere. Come up for a coffee, silly not to, just a black coffee to sober up, and then...

But it didn't stop there. What if her drink had been spiked? What if she was being held against her will? What if something much worse – unimaginable – had happened to her? And he was miles away, in Munich, a six-hour drive, and there was nothing he could do to help her!

Philipp felt like he was going to burst into tears. He steadied himself against the wall of the house. This was appalling. Deeply unprofessional.

Think, Philipp. Think! He could do nothing until he was back tomorrow, anyway. But now he'd gone and promised Frau Schmitt he'd go and drink coffee with her, instead of doing the really important thing: finding Annelie. What a moron! What an absolute idiot he was!

But hang on, perhaps he *could* do something. He had his mobile, didn't he? He could let the boys get on with loading up the van while he made some phone calls. It wasn't an impossible situation.

But first, he'd better clean up. Who knew what he'd got

all down his face in the last few minutes. He was the boss, it was no good going out there with smears down his cheeks. He reached into his pocket for a tissue, and as he did so, he remembered the little flake of green paint, still there, wrapped up in it. He stopped.

Something else was unspooling in his mind. It felt just as real as the scenario with the drinks and the coffee, possibly even more so. He saw Annelie, kicking and flailing, trying to fight off some invisible attacker. He saw her being carried away, still fighting every step of the way. An open-backed sandal dropping from her foot as she kicks out desperately, kicking against anything, the wall, the banister. Green nail polish scraping off on the door frame as she's dragged through the doorway and bundled violently into a car.

Nail polish! Not paint. It was Annelie's nail polish he'd found on the door post. He had a flake of it right there in his pocket.

He felt faint, alternating between hot and cold as the enormity of what might have happened in that quiet neighbourhood hit him square in the face. He'd been an idiot not to see it before.

He knew he had to act, and act now. Annelie, if she was still alive, was in grave danger. But as yet he had no proof, only a tiny fragment of nail polish. Would anyone believe his story? No policeman in Germany would think it enough, certainly not Hannes Schnied, that fat lump sitting there in his office in the Hofheim police station, never lifting a finger!

He needed proof. His brain was racing. A chemists, that's what he needed. There must be one, if not in the village, then somewhere nearby.

Lukas and Holger were coming out of the house with a large crate, about to load it into the waiting van. 'Not there.

Put it in the truck,' he shouted at them.

'What?' said Holger, resting the crate on the van.

'Not in the van,' he cried. 'Over there, in the truck!'

'Okay, boss,' Holger said. 'Whatever you say.'

As they carried the crate back towards the truck, Philipp slammed the rear doors of the van and climbed in behind the steering wheel. 'I'll be back soon. *Ciao!*'

The boys looked at each other. The van was only half full. But it was pointless to argue with Philipp – if he got an idea into his head, he'd act on it, no matter what. So they just shrugged their shoulders and did as instructed. Philipp watched them in the rear-view mirror as he drove off, knowing they'd stop for a fag break as soon as he turned the corner. He didn't care.

After driving through three tiny villages – no more than hamlets, really – along the country road, he finally arrived in a little market town that boasted one small chemist shop. It didn't take him long to find what he was looking for. The shelves of nail polish were lit up from behind, showing off their rainbow colours, from bright neon to pastel. He held his sample up against them. There! That was it. A perfect match. He pulled out the tiny bottle at the front of its row and held it up to the light. The other glass bottles all shuffled down to fill the gap.

The bright green fluid inside the bottle looked like poison. He read the name on the label: 'Apple Blossom'. Misleading. Apple blossoms were white, surely, not green? He handed over six euros and ninety-nine cents to the woman behind the till, getting a suspicious look from her as he did so. He glared at her. If he wanted to paint his nails green, it was no-one's business but his own. He left the shop with his head held high, carefully stowing the small bottle away in his pocket, next to the tissue bearing the original evidence.

As he pulled up once again outside the house where they were packing up, Lukas, Holger and Benjy all turned around and, seeing him, threw their cigarettes nonchalantly down on the ground.

'Back to work then, boys,' he called to them.

'Yes, boss,' came the reply.

EIGHT
Hard-boiled eggs and a negligée

The removals team arrived back in Hofheim at two-thirty the following afternoon. Philipp stopped off at home only to pick up Maschka, a notebook, two hard-boiled eggs (which he always kept in the fridge for any little emergencies), and some small bags, both plastic and paper, for storing any further evidence he might come across.

'Hello, Maschka, old girl – did you miss me?' She was practically hopping up and down at the thought of going on another adventure with him. 'Come on then. No time to waste.'

When she saw Philipp climbing onto his motorbike, Maschka jumped into the sidecar, her tail wagging furiously. It was her favourite way to get about: she loved how the wind made her ears flutter. Philipp kicked the bike into gear, and off they went.

The long drive back from Munich hadn't been at all easy. Philipp had needed to have words with the lads about a precious vase they'd broken, and a couple of picture frames in which the glass had shattered because they hadn't been stacked properly. On top of which, his worries about Annelie had increased with every hour, and it had taken all his reserves of self-control not to burst into tears over the wheel of the six-tonner.

He realised now that he'd not managed to eat anything since breakfast. He was ravenous. At the first red light they came to, Philipp peeled and ate one of the boiled eggs. He'd finished it by the time the light went green, and they shot off again, Maschka giving him a sideways look as if to remind him of the speed limit. He broke it anyway.

As soon as he arrived at Annelie's door, Philipp crouched down to inspect the dent in the doorframe again. There were still a few tiny flakes of nail polish embedded in the wood. He measured the distance from the indentation to the ground. It seemed to fit his hypothesis. It was certainly possible that it had come from Annelie's foot as she'd been carried forcefully from the house. He shuddered at the thought.

He stood up again, and tried to visualise the scene as it might have happened. Where would her assailant have taken her, once out of the house? To a waiting car, presumably. Or… He went across the courtyard to the row of bins that were standing there, all tidily labelled. Nothing of any note there. He walked along the neatly trimmed bushes that bordered the path leading to the road. Aha! There were some broken twigs hanging from one of the bushes. He inspected them closely. They seemed to be fresh, and at a height that ruled out the handiwork of a dog. He nodded grimly and looked at Maschka.

'I'm going to need your help, Maschka, my girl.'

She wagged her tail, and barked twice, as if to say, 'Trust me, I'm up to it.'

He went back to the door and rang the doorbell. It opened almost immediately, and Frau Schmitt was there, beaming at him.

'Philipp! Oh, thank the Lord!'

Noticing the dog alongside him, her face fell. She took a step back into the house.

'It's only Maschka,' he said. 'Do you mind if she comes in? She does get lonely sitting out there, all on her own.'

Reluctantly, Frau Schmitt opened the door wide to let them in.

While she was busy making coffee in the kitchen, Philipp clicked his tongue for Maschka to follow him, and they both padded silently up the stairs. He tried a couple of doors before finding Annelie's bedroom. On a chest of drawers stood several small bottles of nail polish, including a half-full one with 'Apple Blossom' on the label. He pocketed it inside one of his paper evidence bags.

Excellent work, he thought to himself. But he needed more. This was his only chance, while Frau Schmitt was busy with the coffee. He glanced quickly around the room. The bed was made and looked untouched. He stuck his hand underneath her pillow and pulled out... a silky negligée! He lifted it to his face and, feeling a little ashamed of himself, took a sniff. Yes, perfect, that would do. Quickly he stuffed it under his shirt, securing it in place with his belt, and he left the room with Maschka at his heels, as silently as they'd entered it.

They got back to the living room just in time. As the door opened and Frau Schmitt entered with her tray, backwards as usual, he was flicking through a magazine with Maschka at his feet. They both looked up at her sweetly.

'How lovely, Frau Schmitt. Thank you.'

'Welcome,' she said.

She settled down next to him on the sofa, and as he reached for the sugar, she gently placed a hand on his arm. 'I took care of the sugar already,' she said with a delicate smile across her broad features.

Yes, he thought, taking a sip of his coffee – it was exactly as sweet as he liked it. Philipp looked up at her. When she smiled, as she was doing now, she looked a good deal younger. It was hard to tell how old she was, exactly. He'd assumed she was well into her seventies, but now he wasn't so sure. Maybe the way she dressed and behaved made her seem older than she really was. There was no point dwelling on it, he could hardly ask the woman her age without seeming impertinent. What did it matter, anyway?

'Thank you for coming, Herr von Werthern…'

'Philipp, please,' he said, interrupting her. Not without a slight sense of annoyance. It seemed to him that she'd used his surname intentionally, as if she wanted him to insist on greater intimacy between them.

'Philipp,' she repeated, with that coy smile of hers. 'Thank you. I didn't know what to do. When Annelie – Fräulein Janssen, of course – when she didn't come back, I thought of calling the police. But then, what do they know?'

'In my experience, very little,' he agreed.

'I thought to myself, Philipp knows her. He's the man for the job.'

He hardly knew her at all, he thought, but he nodded. 'I'm glad you did. It's very worrying.'

'Do you have the slightest idea where Fräulein Janssen might be?'

Was he imagining it, or was she speaking differently now? The local accent seemed to have slipped away. Or perhaps it was the just the effect of the coffee. He took another sip from his cup.

Maschka looked up at him, and then over at Frau Schmitt, wrinkling her brows as she did so. Philipp thought it made her look quizzical. She'd make a very good prosecutor.

'I have very little to go on,' he began. 'I was hoping you might have something more to tell me.'

'Me?' she said, clearly quite surprised.

'Yes. You seemed worried about something when you called. Something you couldn't discuss over the phone, maybe.'

Frau Schmitt moved her head slowly from side to side. Her expression was deeply serious, all of a sudden. Her face had taken on a greyish tint. 'Well, as you know, I've been working here for years. Two nights in a row she doesn't come home, that's unusual. Never happened before. Naturally, I'm worried.'

It struck Philipp that Frau Schmitt seemed to be in Annelie's house rather a lot. She'd told him she worked here two days a week, more when required – but these days she seemed to be practically living here.

'And then that man outside on the street,' she went on.

'Have you seen him again?' Philipp shot back.

Frau Schmitt shook her head. 'No. Not again. But what if he did something to her? Like he did to Baboo.'

Philipp clenched his jaw. The thought had occurred to him too. It was occurring to him now, and he didn't like it one bit.

'Are you sure you remember nothing else?' he asked, briskly.

'Nothing. Nothing at all.'

From the way she sipped her coffee, Philipp knew he'd come to a dead end. He didn't feel like making small talk, but it seemed like Frau Schmitt had nothing else to give. He felt sure she'd seen something. Perhaps she didn't realise the importance of it, whatever it was. That was often the way in the kind of crime fiction he liked to read: someone would mention something in a perfectly casual way, just by-the-by, and the detective would make a mental note of it, and later on he'd remember it, and it would crack the case wide open.

What he had to do was jog her memory. Perhaps if he

brought the conversation back to where it all started. 'How is Baboo?' he asked. 'Has the paw healed up now?'

'Better,' she replied. 'I shut her in the kitchen, because of the dog.'

'You needn't have worried on Maschka's account,' he said. 'She's very good with cats.' He gave Maschka a reassuring pat on the head, knowing she was likely to take it all personally.

When he looked up again, Frau Schmitt was in tears. Her shoulders were heaving with great sobs, and she'd turned her face away. Philipp felt paralysed. He didn't know what to do. Should he pat her on the back? Give her a hug? Instead, he just handed her a hankie. She took it from him, dabbed her eyes with it, and then blew her nose into it forcefully. That seemed to calm her down nicely.

'Now now,' he said. 'There's no need. I'll find whoever did this, I promise.' And, standing up, he said his goodbyes – with many reassurances and promises to return – and left the house, with Frau Schmitt still clutching his hankie on the sofa.

Making sure the front door was tightly closed behind him, he turned to Maschka. 'Here, girl. Get a sniff of this.'

He pulled out a corner of Annelie's negligée from underneath his shirt, and let Maschka take a good long sniff at it. She responded excitedly, wagging her tail frantically, and giving little whimpers. She must have really taken to Annelie, he thought, and remembered how Annelie had stroked her head while they'd been together in the car. Maschka had deep feelings for certain people, and Annelie seemed to be one of them.

'Search, Maschka, search!' he commanded. Maschka just stood there looking up at him, arching her brows, as if to remind him that she wasn't in fact a bloodhound. But then she dropped her nose to the ground and sniffed at the doorstep with utter professionalism, before turning round and trotting off down the path, nose to the ground, giving every sign of following the scent.

With a jolt of excitement, Philipp went after her. She sniffed her way over to the bushes that he'd investigated earlier, pausing at the place where the twigs were broken to give it her full attention. Then she picked up the trail further along the path, wagging her tail low to the ground, concentrating hard, her nose tracing whatever invisible trail she was finding there.

Philipp followed her around the corner and watched her break into a run along the pavement, until she stopped short at a parked Volvo. She gave a quiet little bark, and began sniffing around at the back of the car, by the boot.

'What have you found?' he said, softly in case any of the neighbours were watching.

Maschka looked up at him with beetling brows. He felt his mouth go dry. She had stopped next to a Volvo that was parked beneath a fir tree, out of sight of the house. There could be a very simple explanation for the scent stopping here, it could be Annelie's car. Even though this was in all likelihood the reason, as a detective he had to take into consideration that there might be a more sinister reason altogether. That was quite literally his job. He went up to it, as casually as he could, and tried the boot. It was locked. The doors were all locked too. There was nothing he could see inside the car that gave any clue as to its owner. If he were to smash one of the windows to get in, it would draw too much attention. Best to sit tight and keep watch.

Almost immediately, though, he realised he wouldn't be able to keep watch without being seen. There was nowhere to hide. Equally, despite the small provisions he'd packed, he was still ravenously hungry. And there was Maschka to think about too. It was no good, he'd have to go home.

Maybe he could come back later and check on developments – though the car might be miles away by then. It was easy to see the advantage of having an entire police department at your disposal when you were working on a case like this. But he was on his own, that was just the way it was. He'd have to make do.

Feeling a bit disheartened, he pulled out his notepad and made a note of the number plate. 'Well done, girl,' he said to Maschka, trying to conceal his disappointment. She beat her tail proudly against the pavement a couple of times. 'You did good.'

NINE
A parcel is delivered

As soon as they were home again, and he'd given Maschka a handful of doggie treats as a reward for her endeavours, Philipp felt himself overcome by a wave of fatigue. He tumbled into bed in the clothes he was wearing and was asleep before his cheek hit the pillow.

After about an hour of untroubled sleep, he was woken by a tugging on his trouser leg. It was Maschka.

'What is it, girl?' he said, groping around for his glasses. Maschka gave a piercing whine. It sounded pretty urgent. He fished about for his red clogs, and slipped them on. He'd rarely seen her so agitated. She knew she wasn't allowed in his bedroom – what had got into her?

Looking down, he saw she was nudging something towards him across the floor. A brown padded envelope. 'Where's that come from, old girl?'

It must have been pushed through the door while he was asleep, and she'd carried it upstairs to him. He picked it up and looked at it more closely.

There was no address on it, only the single word 'PHILIPP' scrawled in permanent marker. Whoever had sent it knew the unusual spelling of his name. It was written in big, childlike block letters, as if to evade any traceable handwriting.

Maschka was now running to and fro across the room between the door and the bed, in a state of high anxiety. 'Okay,' he said. 'I'll open it, if that's what you want.'

Easier said than done. The envelope was wrapped in several layers of brown packing tape, and he couldn't rip it open. He grabbed his house keys and got to work on it with them. It was a good while before he'd severed the last sticky thread and could get it open. Without warning, the contents fell into his lap.

One look was enough.

He nearly fell over Maschka in his hurry to get to the loo. His feet half slipped out of the clogs, and their hard rims cut into his arches, but he didn't stop until he reached the toilet bowl. He hadn't eaten much. It was only bile that came up.

He flushed it away and rinsed his mouth out with tap water. His pale stubbly face looked back at him from the mirror. He had that old, familiar feeling in the pit of his stomach: the feeling he'd had whenever one of his children had been in danger. His legs felt weak and wobbly, and an ice-cold lump of panic slid down from his mouth into his belly and lay there heavily.

He looked at the ghost of himself in the mirror and uttered a single word: 'Shit!'

His brain was working feverishly, but whoever was controlling it, it didn't seem to be him. Without really understanding what he was doing, he opened the mirrored bathroom cabinet and took out a pair of tweezers. He had no idea who'd left them in there, but they seemed to be what he was looking for.

Back in the bedroom now, he had to focus hard on not being sick again as he used the tweezers to pick up the object that had fallen out of the envelope. He slid it carefully into one of his evidence bags.

Once the bag was sealed, his stomach started to calm down. The nausea receded a little. He carried the bag over to his bedside, so he could have a look at it under the light.

It was someone's little toe, neatly severed at the root. Its nail was painted green. Apple Blossom green.

Inside him a storm of fear and anger was raging. Where was she? Who'd taken her? Where was she being held? What was this supposed to mean, sending him her little toe? First Baboo, now her. Where was this going to end? What sick mind was behind all this?

The questions kept coming and coming, and there weren't any answers. Why had the toe been sent to *him*? Why not to some relative of hers, one of her boyfriends in the city, someone with money? It didn't make any sense. Was he being mocked? Was someone trying to show what a poor detective he was? If so, they were certainly succeeding. It was a game of cat-and-mouse, and he didn't have a clue how it was supposed to be played.

If they were after a ransom or something like that, surely they'd have sent him a message? He looked in the envelope again to see if there was anything still inside. There wasn't. Nothing on the outside either, apart from his name in those big clumsy letters. He lifted the envelope to his nose and sniffed it. It smelled faintly of iron, probably from the blood. Feeling sick again, he dropped the envelope on the floor, lay back on the bed, and stared up at the ceiling.

A loud bark from Maschka brought him to his senses. She was right, there was no time to lose. They had to find Annelie.

He clattered down the stairs into his office and started up the computer with feverish panic-driven fingers. While the computer took its agonising time to boot up, he went back up to the kitchen and poured himself a tall glass of Coke with plenty of ice. He needed to mask the foul taste in his mouth. And he was going to need the caffeine.

Back in front the computer, he fished his notebook out of his pocket and tapped in the Volvo's registration number. He hit return. Up on the screen, a 'loading' icon started to spin.

'Come on, faster, faster!'

Finally, the results came up. There were some details for vehicles with similar numbers on various used car websites, but none for the one he needed. He scrolled down. Nothing. No help at all. In frustration, he hit the keyboard with the flat of his hand, and the computer screen went blank. 'Useless piece of junk!'

With a trembling hand he took a long drink from the cold glass of Coke. It did him no good whatsoever.

What now? If this was a crime drama, he'd be able to call up an ally in the police department who'd be able to look it up for him, and he'd have an address in no time at all. Was this the moment to call Hannes Schnied at the Hofheim police station and come clean about everything? He pictured the fat cop leaning back in his chair, telling him to start right from the beginning. No way, there was no time. There had to be another way.

He had it! The licensing office. Of course, they must have a database of all the number plates in the area. It would be easy for them to find out who the car was registered to. The only problem was, it would be classified information. They wouldn't just hand out an address to anyone who happened to enquire, would they? Would they?

Moments later he was behind the wheel of the turquoise Opel, Maschka beside him in the passenger seat, tyres squealing as they took the corner at speed, heading towards town.

This time Maschka had to wait on her own in the car, as there was no Annelie to wait with her. Philipp's mood was grim as he entered the licensing office, and it didn't lighten when he saw there was an even longer queue than usual. As he waited in line, he could feel the evidence bag in his breast pocket, with its tiny contents pressing against his chest. It felt like an anchor weighing on his heart. He began to think that the other people waiting in the queue could see what was in there. Any minute they'd call the police, and he'd be dragged off to explain himself to Hannes Schnied. All he could think about was the moment a blade had come down on Annelie's little toe, lopping it off onto the bare floor.

Philipp leant over the plastic counter and smiled as charmingly as he could at the woman behind it. He wasn't going to waste his only chance.

He knew the woman quite well, from years of frequenting the licensing office on behalf of clients. Her name was Jennifer. She liked dogs, and had a real soft spot for golden retrievers in general, and for Maschka in particular. She liked to spoil Maschka with treats she kept behind her desk. They'd often chatted away, she and the dog, and she seemed to like telling Maschka all the details of her personal life – details she probably wouldn't have told just anyone who walked into the office.

This was how Philipp knew that Jennifer was single, liked Chinese food and ten-pin bowling, and had some problems with a recurring summer cold.

He made sure now to ask after her health, hoped she wasn't suffering too badly this year, and wondered if she had anything exciting planned for after work. She asked after Maschka, and he told her that she was quite well, though he hadn't brought her in today as he'd seen the office was a little busy.

'You bring her in next time,' Jennifer said. 'I'll have

something for her.'

'You're too good,' he said, and then, slipping across the counter a piece of paper on which he'd written the Volvo's registration number, asked if she might do him the tiniest favour.

She hesitated only for the fraction of a second. Then, smiling, she got up and went to have a look in the archive.

Philipp drummed his fingers on the counter, waiting. It only took a minute. When she returned, she pushed the piece of paper over to him. He could see there was a name handwritten on it. He flashed her a brilliant smile.

He glanced down at the paper, and all the colour drained from his face. He felt as if his heart had just stopped. His mouth went dry.

He looked up at Jennifer again. Trying to keep his voice level and calm, he said: 'I wonder, would you be able to find the address for me as well, please?'

She looked surprised. 'I'm not really supposed to,' she stuttered. 'But since it's you, I don't see the harm.'

The seconds stretched into eternity. The little bag in his breast pocket began to throb painfully. He felt sure that people were looking at him suspiciously, and it was only a matter of time before the cops pulled up outside…

'There. That should be everything you need,' she said, handing him another piece of paper.

Without looking down at it, he thanked her, wished her a pleasant evening, and left the building on legs that felt like they'd give way if he had to cross the road. Fortunately, he'd parked right outside.

TEN

The dragon's lair

A click. Then the door to the flat swung open without a sound.

It was dark inside, and there was a strange smell. Chalky and damp, with a sickly-sweet top-note that might be some sort of perfume, or perhaps incense sticks, or air freshener.

He was standing in a narrow corridor. The sparse light falling through the open door from the hallway fell on what little there was in the way of furnishings. Two jackets hanging from a coat rack. A narrow bookshelf with very few books, a bowl of loose change on the top. A pair of boots. A rolled-up umbrella. That was all.

Carefully, Philipp edged further into the flat. It was perfectly quiet. Only an electric buzz in the air, or was he imagining that?

He didn't dare switch on a light, he had no idea if there was anyone at home. The darkness inside suggested there wasn't, but what if someone was hiding, waiting for him? He reached into his pocket, grabbed his phone and switched on the torch function.

There were three doors opening off the corridor. One to the left, one to the right and one just opposite the front door, slightly to the side.

He slipped off his clogs and picked them up, so he could continue barefoot. Opening the door on the left, he shone his torch around the room. The beam travelled across a small, modestly furnished kitchen. There was a Formica table with a magazine on it, a kettle, a glass jar with teabags inside, and a bowl of sugar. On the wall, a poster of the sun going down over the sea. The wallpaper was wipe-clean and egg-yolk yellow. Even by torchlight everything seemed extremely clean. Bland. Ordinary. Exactly the way he'd expected Frau Schmitt's kitchen to be.

Had his instincts been wrong? Had he made a terrible mistake? When he'd seen her name on the piece of paper Jennifer had handed him at the licensing office, his first reaction had been shock. And then it was as if the penny had dropped. Of course, it was Frau Schmitt all along! It had to be. She was always there hanging around in Annelie's house. She certainly had the opportunity. And as for motive, she was probably nursing some grievance or other. Perhaps she was scared Annelie would get rid of her, and she'd have to go back to serving pretzels at Frankfurt rail station. She'd do anything to avoid that, blackmail even. It all seemed to fall into place.

So he'd come straight here, to her little flat in Kelkheim, without much of a plan. And as soon as he'd pulled up outside, he'd known how he was going to get in. The block was almost identical to one he'd done a removals job on, only a month ago. That day, he'd locked himself out of the place by accident, but Holger had known how to get back in. He was handy like that, was Holger.

But now, seeing Frau Schmitt's spotless little kitchen, her little glass jar of teabags with the little sugar bowl beside it, all neat and precise and bland, he thought he must be deluding himself. And there was nothing suspicious about a cleaner parking her car outside her employer's house: it's what she was bound to do. Maschka had just picked up some trail or other, and followed it all the way to Frau Schmitt's car. What a damned fool he'd been.

Still, he was here now. He'd broken into her flat, so he'd better see it through. He owed it to Annelie.

He left the kitchen, closing the door softly behind him, and went over to the second door, pushing it open carefully with his fingertips. The sickly-sweet smell intensified. It made him feel light-headed.

Philipp swallowed hard. He concentrated on his breathing. In… Out… Deep, steady breaths. He wasn't going to faint. Not now, not here.

He directed the torch beam onto the opposite wall, and the moment he looked up, he stopped breathing again. He had an impulse to run. In the unsteady light from the torch, he found he was looking at himself. Specifically, a life-size poster image of himself, aged eighteen or nineteen, young and slim, in a white floor-length coat, leaning against his motorbike, with a smile on his lips, looking at someone just out of shot. The picture was taken from a low angle, and in the background you could just about make out the asphalt stairs that led up to his old secondary school, the Gesamtschule am Rosenberg in Hofheim. Beneath the poster, on a chest of drawers, two incense sticks were standing in a glass jar, their tips glowing, sending thin wreaths of smoke curling upwards and making the whole room reek of their sickly perfume.

Gathering the last shreds of his willpower, he forced himself to walk across the room, towards the makeshift altar. Right in the middle of it was a plate with three small balls arranged in a triangle. Philipp peered closely at them, and realised they were each made from one of the red-and-gold Niederegger Marzipan wrappers he knew so well, rolled up in exactly the way he'd always done. It sent a shiver down his spine.

Gingerly, he pulled open one of the drawers of the chest. In it were hundreds of clear plastic zip-up bags, each clearly labelled and ordered. He pulled one of them out to take a closer look. It contained a glass Coca-Cola bottle, now empty. Written on the label were the enigmatic words 'Hofheim, MTS, 1976'. Another bag contained an empty envelope stamped with the words 'We will do it': the motto of the Gothaer insurance company, where he'd worked for several years. On the bag was a label, neatly inscribed 'Mainzer Straße, June 1989 (stamp licked)'.

He replaced the bags quickly in the drawer, feeling his head start to spin. He was reeling, and had to press both hands on the top of the chest of drawers to support himself. He wished he'd brought Maschka with him, and cursed his decision to leave her in the car, thinking she'd be a hindrance. He could have done with her beside him now.

He screwed up his courage and opened the next drawer down. This one was crammed full of photographs, thousands of them, all with one thing in common: they were all of him. Some were out of focus, while in many of them there was only a glimpse of him – the back of his head, or a bit of his coat. Some had been taken with a long-distance lens, others in close-up, or from a strange angle, with bits of foreground intruding. There were pictures of him standing outside on the street, walking in the woods, driving a car, or on his motorbike. There were even pictures that had clearly been taken through the window of his own house. These showed him cooking, or reading, staring at his computer screen, or scraping dog food into Maschka's bowl. There were pictures that showed him at fifteen, and pictures that seemed to have been taken last week. In many of them Maschka appeared too, and in some she was even staring directly into the camera. Philipp shuddered. He remembered once when they'd been out walking and Maschka had stopped suddenly and stared into the thickets, growling from deep in her throat. He'd thought nothing of it at the time. It was only a squirrel or a rabbit, he'd assumed. Oh, Maschka, his clever, loyal dog! She'd known all along!

It was clear now. The answers to his questions lay here, in this flat. The realisation that she'd been following him all his life, since his days at school, hit him like a physical blow. The last piece of the puzzle slotted into place: she'd been his classmate! She had been in his year! Martina Schmitt. Of course. He'd known her for fifty years, and simply hadn't recognised her. All these years since school, she'd never even crossed his mind – while clearly he'd been on hers, constantly.

Now that he was standing in her flat looking at the indisputable evidence of her obsession, he suddenly found long-forgotten memories of her crowding into his mind. A young Martina watching him through thick, slightly fogged glasses. Her gaze unobtrusive, but taking in every detail. He'd always thought she was away with the fairies, forever staring at something, thinking inscrutable thoughts. The thoughts she must have been having! He'd never bothered to find out. She'd been inconsequential to him. And now he'd paid the price.

Everything that had happened, had happened because of him. The cat had lost its paw because of him. Annelie had disappeared, all because of him.

A new image came to him, jolting him out of his memories. Annelie, tied up and gagged in some hideaway somewhere. Where could she be? Anywhere. She might even be at her own home still. In the cellar. Or the attic.

No, he thought. It couldn't be that. He felt sure, from the nail polish on the door frame and the trail that led to Frau

Schmitt's car, that she'd been taken from there. There must be something in this flat that would tell him where Annelie was hidden. And he had to find it, fast.

Moving quickly now, but still as quietly as he could, he shone his torchlight about the room, raking its beam over the walls, looking for any further door. There was none. He went out into the corridor and tried the only remaining door. It was a bathroom, tiled throughout. No way to hide anything there. And the kitchen too was a dead-end.

Feeling a mounting sense of dread, he returned to the one room in the house that kept nagging at him: the one with the shrine devoted to him. If Annelie was hidden anywhere, it would be here, along with all the other trophies of a lifetime of obsessive devotion. She would be the most precious offering of all.

He put the phone down on the altar, propped up, so the torchlight shone against the walls, and then ran the fingers of both hands over the surface of the wallpaper, feeling for cracks or hidden joins. He knocked gently on the walls with his knuckles, listening for a hollow sound that might give away a secret door. Nothing. Everything seemed solid and impenetrable. He'd inspected the entire room, and had to admit there were no hiding spaces. Disappointed, he turned to go, already thinking about his next steps. Perhaps he should drive back to Annelie's, see if there was anything more to be found there.

He was at the door, ready to leave, when he heard a sound. He froze. Was someone coming up the stairs? No, it had come from behind him, from inside the room. A faint scratching sound. Mice? Philipp turned back, listening. There, once again, the faintest sound. It seemed to be coming from behind the chest of drawers. Of course! He leapt across the room and used his shoulder to shove aside the heavy piece of furniture. And there it was, hidden behind it:

a small door.

'Annelie,' he called, and there was the sound again, a rustling, only louder now. And along with it something like a muffled squeaking. He took hold of the doorknob and rattled the door, but it was sturdier than it looked and wouldn't yield. Damn. Where was the key? He ran his fingers through his hair in desperation, urging himself to think, think carefully. Maybe Frau Schmitt carried the key on her person, for safekeeping. He wouldn't put it past her. It might even give her a thrill, dangling it on a chain next to her skin. If so, he hadn't a hope.

An image of Smaug the dragon flashed into his head, that terrifying creature sitting on its great pile of treasure, its red eye opening little by little as the diminutive Hobbit entered its lair. Was this a trap? Had it been set for him a long time ago? If there was one thing Martina Schmitt knew how to do, it was to be patient. She'd been waiting fifty years for this. And she was meticulous enough to hatch an elaborate plan, that much was clear from the way she'd collected those samples, labelled them all, poured so many hours of her life into this. She was an opponent to be reckoned with, and he was running out of time.

He went through the entire flat once again, looking for something that might be the key to the hidden door. But he quickly began to lose hope. She was too scrupulous and tidy, there were very few places to look.

Almost at the point of giving up, he remembered the bowl in the hallway, the one full of loose change. Yes, there were keys in it too! He grabbed the entire bowl and took it back into the room so he could try each of the keys in the door. It had to be one of them, it just had to be!

At the third attempt, one turned in the lock. The door opened with soft, well-oiled click. He flashed his torch around inside. There was a small, dusty chamber, half full of boxes. And there was something else. He shone his torch back towards the furthest corner. Yes! Something there. A leg… a pair of legs, drawn up under a ragged mat of hair. Blonde hair! He barely recognised her. She looked nothing like the Annelie he remembered. She was a pale, haggard wraith, her clothes filthy and tattered, one bare foot wrapped in a soiled bandage, a cloth tied tight around her mouth, her eyes blinking at the sudden blinding light. She tried to shuffle towards him, not knowing who it was, only trusting it was nothing worse than had come at her before.

'It's me,' he said in an urgent whisper. 'Philipp!'

From her gagged mouth came a torrent of squawks and moans.

'Wait,' he said. 'Keep quiet. I'll get you out, but you've got to stay quiet.'

He got to work, removing the gag from her mouth, releasing her bindings. She was silent now, watching him with startled, unbelieving eyes.

'Are you going to be able to walk?' he asked, looking at the cruel strap-marks around her wrists and ankles. She nodded. There was little alternative, anyway. If they were going to get out of this place, she'd have to get to her feet.

They crawled on hands and knees back out into the room, out of that horrifying chamber. Once there, he was able to haul her to her feet. She grimaced with pain, and hung like a dead weight from his shoulder, but she managed first one step, then two. She gritted her teeth and kept going. Out into the corridor. Then along the corridor. There it was, the front door, waiting for them, and beyond it lay safety, an end to this terrible nightmare…

They stopped dead in their tracks. They'd both heard it. Footsteps in the corridor outside, coming to a halt right on the other side of the front door. Keys jangling. Turning in the lock.

Philipp didn't stop to think. He dragged Annelie through the door on their right, into the kitchen, just as the front door opened. Mistake. There was nowhere to hide in here. They pressed themselves against the wall, praying she would go on down the corridor. Philipp looked at Annelie, her eyes wide with fear. It seemed like she was about to drop to the floor. He pushed his body against hers to stop her falling, to take up as little space as possible. They held their breath. Philipp could hear Martina Schmitt's breathing, laboured after climbing the stairs. If she came into the kitchen and turned on the light, they were lost. That would be it. She would be ready and armed, Philipp was sure of it. If she went on past the kitchen, there'd be a chance. A tiny one, but a chance. They'd be discovered anyway, that much was certain. He'd left the door to the chamber open, the chest of drawers pushed to one side. And his clogs! He'd dropped them in the middle of the room. He could hardly have left a more obvious calling card.

They had only seconds left before they were discovered. His body pressed against hers, holding her upright. Their faces so close together he could feel her breath on his cheek. He could see she was looking at the sink, looking at it with a desperate, dangerous desire, and he realised how thirsty she must be, her lips so dry, and cracks in the corners of her mouth. She needed water almost more than she needed to be free. He grew scared she might even trade freedom for one glass of water, and he shook his head firmly. No. Hold on. You've got to hold on.

The footsteps were approaching down the corridor. Philipp tried to recall the exact layout of the flat, where the walls were and the openings, the angles. It was a confused jumble in his mind. They heard a door being opened and they both flinched in readiness, but it wasn't the kitchen door. There was a moment's pause, and then the sound of clothes rustling, a zipper, and, unmistakeably, the sound of someone having a pee. This was their chance! Philipp grabbed Annelie's hand and squeezed it hard. He looked her in the eyes and indicated with a movement of the head that they needed to make their move. She nodded and the two of them inched into the corridor and crept silently past the toilet door towards the front door. They reached it just as the toilet was being flushed. Philipp pushed the handle down, opened the door, and they were outside, in the corridor.

The final dash had cost Annelie all of her strength, and she dropped to her knees. She could go no further. Philipp bent down, took hold of her arms and heaved her onto his back. He managed to settle her into a kind of piggyback. Not sure how long he'd be able to keep her there, he set off towards the head of the stairs, barefoot, tottering beneath his load.

He took the stairs two at a time, risking everything. If he stumbled now, they'd end up in a heap at the bottom, as good as dead. He kept listening for the sound of someone pursuing them from the top of the stairs. She couldn't be far behind. He couldn't hear anything except his own breathing, coming thick and fast. His lungs felt like they were about to burst.

And then somehow, they were out in the open, under the night sky, pounding along the pavement. He didn't know how they'd managed it, he couldn't even remember how they'd got out of the building.

There was his car. Ten metres away. Five. If he could just reach it before Martina came out of the building. He'd left it unlocked as he always did, but he still had to get Annelie into it, and he wasn't at all sure how he was going to do that.

They reached the car and still no one had come out of the building behind them. There was a chance. He slid

Annelie off his back and propped her against the car as he flung open the passenger door. She seemed to recover herself a little because she stepped forward and put one foot into the car, and then fell forward onto the passenger seat. Maschka, who'd been sitting in that seat herself, startled by everything that was going on, made way for her, jumping across to the back seats of the car, and then turning back to give Annelie's face a lick. Philipp slammed the passenger door shut and started sprinting round to the driver's side.

At that moment, Martina Schmitt burst out of the building. As he reached the driver's door, Philipp saw her clock them. He didn't stop to see any more. He flung himself behind the wheel and jammed the key into the ignition.

The Opel was temperamental. One of two things would happen now. Either he'd fire the ignition, and the engine would hiccup, and then groan, and eventually start ticking over. Or it wouldn't start at all.

A third thing happened instead. The Opel started up straight away with a fine throaty roar.

Philipp looked in the rear-view mirror and saw Martina Schmitt, her face red and puckered with rage, foaming at the mouth, brandishing a weapon. With clenched teeth, he pushed the accelerator to the floor, and the car shot forward, just as Martina discharged her weapon. There was a loud crash as the rear windscreen shattered into a thousand fragments on the back seat. Annelie screamed. Philipp looked again in the mirror, and there was nothing between him and the cold night sky, no glass left at all, only Martina's face receding now as they sped away down the road.

'What happened?' yelped Annelie, next to him. 'Did she shoot at us?'

Philipp shook his head. 'It's all right,' he said. 'She didn't have a gun.'

He took one last look in the mirror. He could no longer

see Frau Schmitt. There on the back seat, in a heap of broken glass, sat a single red leather Danish clog.

'We're safe now,' he said, as they drove into the night.

ELEVEN
A year later

'Sorry, Maschka. You'll have to wait outside.'

Philipp's first impression of the building was its smell. Cabbages and cleaning products. He was following a man who unlocked several doors with a heavy set of keys and brought him to a light-filled hall. There were tables and chairs dotted around. People sitting, talking.

At a table over in the corner sat Frau Schmitt. She was staring down at the tabletop in front of her.

'Good morning,' he said. She didn't look up. He pulled out the chair opposite her and sat down. 'How are you, Martina?'

Her eyes behind their thick glasses slid carefully across the table and came to a rest somewhere around the second-highest button on Philipp's red-and-black lumberjack shirt. He could see her face more clearly now. There was a hint of curiosity there. And suspicion, too, perhaps. She was clearly burning to know why he'd come, but she wasn't going to risk asking him. She couldn't even meet his eyes.

Keeping her lips pressed tightly shut, she inhaled audibly through her nose and folded her arms across her chest.

'I hear they're moving you to another prison tomorrow,'

he said. She gave a barely perceptible nod. 'Are you going far?'

She shrugged. 'Freistaat Thüringen,' she muttered.

He nodded. 'They have an open prison there, don't they? That's good. Better than here, maybe.' He smiled at her. She shrugged again.

'I can still visit, if you'd like me to.'

She looked up, and for the first time looked him straight in the eyes. 'Why? You haven't so far.'

She was right. This was the first time he'd been to see her. He just hadn't had the time. Life had been busy, unexpectedly. A lot had happened. He wasn't sure yet if he was going to tell her.

'I'd like to come and visit you, if that's ok.'

'What for?' she shot back, her eyes narrowing. 'Why'd you want to do a thing like that? What's left to say?'

Philipp was rarely lost for words, but he found he was now. He looked down at the tabletop between them, and scratched at its chipped surface with his fingernail.

The facts had all come out at the trial. Martina Schmitt had always struggled in life. Ever since school, she'd cut herself off from people, always living alone, doing a succession of temporary jobs, never fitting in, never really wanting to. She lived for one thing only: her obsession with him. It kept her busy. Gave her a sense of purpose. She devoted almost all of her time to it. The results were laid bare in the courtroom for everyone to see: crate after crate of it, newly bagged and labelled, even though she'd bagged and labelled it all herself, right from the start.

Her parents had died one after the other in quick succession while she was in her teens. She'd been left alone in the world, even more alone than she'd been during her lonely childhood. Whenever things got too much for her, she would cut herself. She cut herself in places she could hide from the world. She enjoyed seeing her own blood, and the pain gave her a feeling of release that came instantly, every time. She exalted in the pain, though it was all too brief. She had to go on cutting herself, again and again. The pictures were shown in court. Philipp had had to look away.

She lost her job at the pretzel stall at Frankfurt station when her manager caught her self-harming during her lunchbreak, round the back by the air-conditioning units. Shortly after that she'd seen Annelie's advert for a cleaner, and had been surprised when she'd got the job – though working at the pretzel stall had taught her how to make a decent cup of coffee, and Fräulein Janssen liked her coffee.

But working for Annelie had made her wretched. She conceived a morbid jealousy of her employer – so young, so beautiful, and so at peace with the world – and had begun to imagine that Annelie was sleeping around, using her sexual allure to captivate men in a way that she, plain old Martina Schmitt, could never hope to do. She felt she had to put a stop to it. She wanted to hurt Annelie in some way.

She began with the cat. She didn't dislike the cat in any way. She was fond of cats, had even had one herself when she was young, though it had been knocked down by a careless driver and had later died of its injuries, despite everything her father – who was a veterinary surgeon – could do for it. She didn't want Baboo to die, she just wanted Annelie to stay at home for once and care for it, to stop seeing all those imaginary men.

So she'd ground up a sleeping pill and mixed it in with Baboo's food. Then she'd taken the comatose cat into the bathroom and carefully removed her paw with a scalpel. She knew how to do it, she'd kept her father's old textbooks. She even knew how to stitch it up properly. It wasn't difficult. She thought anyone might be able to do it, and said so in court. People these days underestimated their own capabilities. And she found they always underestimated her too.

Doing what she'd done to Baboo had made her feel alive and powerful, and it had been worth it. But the feeling didn't last long. It ended the moment Philipp walked in through the door.

The court heard all about Martina's love for Philipp, at precisely the same time that Philipp was learning about it. She'd fallen in love with him when they were both twelve years old. She'd never lost sight of him since, not once, though she'd been too shy to let him know. It was better kept a secret, anyway. It made her life richer. Worth living.

When he'd walked in through Annelie's door and failed to recognise her, Martina's world had fallen apart. Up until that moment, she'd entertained a fantasy that he felt the same about her but was simply too shy to confess his love. She dreamt of the day he would overcome his shyness, and their life together would begin. She pictured to herself the fateful day, the knock on the door, the blissful realisation that everything was now in its rightful place. She longed for that day to come.

Then the knock on the door did come, and the bubble had burst. She could no longer pretend: she, Martina Schmitt, was nothing to him. In his eyes, she'd never even existed.

Philipp had testified in court that he'd always found faces difficult to remember. He was aware he had a blindness in that area. Under normal circumstances, he'd have been mortified to discover that he'd failed to recognise an old classmate, but these were far from normal circumstances. More than forty years had elapsed since he'd last set eyes on her, and she looked so different now. They both did, no doubt, but it had been much less time since she'd last seen him. Hardly any time at all.

She'd explained in court how she'd come to kidnap

Annelie. She'd done it after seeing her employer kissing Philipp, a man she'd met only hours before. The man that she herself had been in love with all her life. It was so easy for Annelie, she could have any man she wanted. And she was choosing Philipp. She was snatching him away. It just wasn't fair. She must be made to pay.

The abduction itself was a simple matter, and she was happy to explain it to the court. First of all, there were the crushed-up sleeping pills dissolved in a cappuccino. Then, when Annelie had collapsed so conveniently on top of an antique rug, all Martina had had to do was roll her up inside it, like a sushi roll, and carry the whole thing out to the car. When the judge expressed some doubt about this, saying he found it hard to believe she'd carried it without the help of an accomplice, she said no, she'd acted entirely alone. People were always underestimating her strength. The woman who lived next door, Frau Kaaserer, was able to corroborate this when she was called upon to testify. She appeared in the witness stand in high heels and extravagant make-up, and declared that she'd seen Frau Schmitt coming out of the house, carrying the rug over one shoulder. She remembered making a remark about it, too, and Frau Schmitt had told her it was only an old carpet that needed cleaning. Frau Kaaserer didn't ask any more about it, since it wasn't her business what people did with their carpets.

With Annelie out of the way, Martina had tried her best to make Philipp see things in the right light. She played on his concern for Annelie, inviting him over for coffee. That was a wonderful time for her, and for a few hours that afternoon she thought it would be the turning point in her life. But it turned out not to be. Nothing ever turned out the way she hoped.

Fearing that she was losing his interest, and that he may even be on to her, she invented the story of the man in the baseball cap. But it wasn't enough. When Philipp walked out of the door, she knew she had to do something else, something bold, or she'd lose him forever. The solution had come to her when she'd been clearing the coffee things away. Philipp had left one of the marzipans unopened on the plate. His favourite Niederegger Marzipans! Something must be wrong for him to leave it. And looking at it there, a single fat lozenge alone on the plate, she thought how much it looked like a little marzipan finger. Or even a toe.

Perhaps if she sent him Annelie's toe, he'd start to take this all a little more seriously.

They lapped this up in the public gallery, the lot of them, and she seemed to enjoy the attention it got her. Attention that she'd been starved of for the whole of her life. As she explained to the court, in meticulous detail, how she'd gone about severing the toe, she'd looked across the courtroom, right at Philipp, who was sitting next to his beloved Annelie. She looked at him then, and never once looked at him again, all the way through the rest of the trial, right up to the moment she was sentenced. And even then, she went down without so much as a glance at him.

She was looking at him now though, as he sat there in the visiting room, picking away at the tabletop with his fingernail.

'Martina,' he began, withdrawing his hand as it began to tremble. 'I came to say something to you.'

'Well,' she said. 'Now's your chance.'

'I came to say... I'm sorry.' He put his hand down in his lap, safely under the table where it couldn't be seen. 'Sorry that I didn't notice you, and what you were going through. It must have been dreadful, loving someone for all that time, and not being noticed. For what it's worth – and this is not to say it's anything like what *you* went through – I do know what it's like. Loving, I mean. And not being loved in return.'

'At least you've been loved,' she said, with an edge in her voice.

'I have,' he said. 'I've been extraordinarily lucky.'

'No, Philipp. It's not just a matter of luck. Some of us are born to be loved. And some of us… are not.'

He glanced up at her. There was a glint in her eyes. A terrible, self-pitying triumph.

'Martina, I think you must just give it some time,' he said.

She heaved a long, weary sigh. 'In here, Philipp, time is all I have.'

He nodded. It was no use arguing. What he'd come to tell her would have to wait. He pushed back his chair and stood up, saying quickly, 'I'll come and see you again.'

'In Freistaat Thüringen?'

'It's not so far. I don't mind a journey. I'll come if you'd like me to.'

She thought for a moment, then quietly nodded. 'Okay, then. Yes.'

He thought he saw a tear in the corner of her eye, and so, to save her any embarrassment, he said a hurried goodbye. Then he turned and walked over to the door without looking back.

Outside, Maschka greeted him like he was an old pal who'd just served twenty years.

'Easy, girl. Calm down.' He patted her on the head, and she looked up at him with soft, enquiring eyes. 'What's that?' he said. 'No, I couldn't tell her. Don't look at me like that, I just couldn't. Okay, okay, I'll tell her the next time. Now, can we go?'

He untied her, and they walked off together to where he'd parked the car.

EPILOGUE

A few weeks later there was a party to celebrate Philipp's sixty-first birthday. Now that life had settled into its course once again he wanted to make up for the sixtieth, which he hadn't felt like celebrating in style under the circumstances. He had invited all his friends and family, about a hundred guests in all.

He'd hired the courtyard of The Barn, a little place between Hofheim and Lorsbach, and had opted to do the catering and everything else himself, with the help of his housemates. By early evening, the place was abuzz as everyone packed themselves in around a set of mismatched tables, tucking into the food he'd lovingly prepared. It all began with his signature dish, the famous avocado sherry soup, served out of a battered tureen by Michi and Youssef.

The evening was mild and a gentle breeze blew through the courtyard, bobbing the balloons up and down and making the fire torches flicker. It all seemed quite magical. Music drifted over from somewhere, Philipp didn't know where – perhaps Laura had brought her guitar. There was the sound of laughter, conviviality, and the clink of spoons on china bowls. He looked around the place with satisfaction.

Over there were the four Schlumpas, his grown-up children, come from far and wide to celebrate with him. Their mothers too were here, gossiping together at one of the corner tables and giggling. In amongst the grown-ups, running wild, were countless children, his own grandchildren and the children and grandchildren of his friends, ducking between the tables, chasing Maschka, playing tag, tugging at shirt sleeves, exploring every hidden corner of the place. It filled his heart with joy.

There, by the drinks table, were the boys from his removals team, Holger, Benjy and Lukas. They seemed to be having a good time, except – thwack! – Holger hit Benjy over the head with a rolled-up serviette… But they were both laughing about it, so it was probably fine.

In another corner, his surgeon friend Christoph was bent over a piece of paper with a furrowed brow, mumbling to himself. Practising his speech, no doubt. He took it all so seriously, and always wanted to say a few words, whatever the occasion. Though, often as not, he was called away to some medical emergency just in time.

All his closest friends in one place, and all because he was turning sixty-one!

He turned to Annelie, sitting beside him, and gave her a kiss. She looked so happy tonight, and he didn't think he'd ever seen her so beautiful. That slight look of anxiety she'd carried around with her for months had now almost completely vanished. She still wouldn't wear sandals, preferring to keep her foot covered up even on the hottest of days, but her complexion had fully recovered. If she had bags under her eyes, it wasn't from any residual trauma – it was just that she'd been up most of the previous night with their baby daughter Emma.

He hadn't expected to become a dad again. Not at his stage of life. It had taken him by surprise. Not one of those surprises you try to wish away – Philipp loved children, and always had room for them in his life. He just hadn't thought it possible. But now that Emma was here, and making her presence felt in every way, he knew it just had to be. He loved her to bits.

And Emma, for her part, loved being the centre of attention. She revelled in it. She took it for granted that every grown-up she ever encountered was related to her in some way, either an aunt, a great-uncle, a distant cousin or one of her big half-sisters' children (she didn't yet know there were such things as nephews or nieces, though she had them in abundance). She was sitting there now, in Annelie's lap, looking around at everything and everyone with her big brown eyes, like it was her own birthday rather than his. Indeed, everyone said she took after her father. They did both love a party.

Philipp was enjoying his sixties, it had to be said. He didn't feel at all old. He kept himself busy, he'd never been busier. Word had spread of his success in private investigating, and now potential clients were seeking him out, so many he had to turn some of them away (the ones who'd lost a cat or mislaid a piece of jewellery). Annelie teased him about living life like a teenager, bursting with energy for all his exciting projects but in fact it turned out she herself looked a lot younger than her age. She was older than his eldest daughter after all, which was a great relief to all parties. And Emma had come along quickly to seal the deal.

The whole courtyard was vibrating with life. With well-lived life. Maschka came over and sat down at his feet, relieved to have escaped the attentions of the younger party guests for a minute or two. She too looked round at the happy throng, as if to say, 'Well, they seem to be enjoying themselves.' Philipp patted her head affectionately, and when he looked up, his middle daughter was just stepping up to the microphone, smoothing out a piece of paper on which she'd written her speech. The musician was asked to break off for a while, and the speech began, the first of the evening, all of them about Philipp, the accidental detective.

When it had finished, the applause rang out around the courtyard, Maschka gave a loud approving bark, and everyone shouted in unison:

'Three cheers for Philipp! For Philipp! For Philipp!'

Acknowledgements

Thank you to everyone who made this book possible: to my family in Germany and my family in London, and all my many friends who supported me during the writing and the translation process – you know who you are! Thank you for space and time to James, Marlene and Luka. For practical support and advice, thank you to Matt Applewhite, Tim Digby-Bell, Ian Higham, Sarah Lambie and Sarah Liisa Wilkinson. Thank you, Ana Ilic, Eleanor Lowenthal and Teresa Szechter for support in getting the book out in the UK. Thank you to Emma Fischer, Lily McLeish, Piers Torday and Julia Woelke von Werthern for reading, editing and helping with the German version. Thank you, Nicole Dietzel, Perdita Fitzgerald, Kim Otto, Catarin Roeser, Verena Silvanus, Karoline Sinur and Annegret Weil for support in getting the German version out in Germany and making it a success. And huge thanks to my wonderful and patient editor Robin Booth, to Jodi Gray for typesetting and making this book look beautiful on the inside, and to Andrew Davis for the brilliant cover design.

Author image © Jon Holloway | www.jonholloway.co.uk

Tamara von Werthern is a German-British writer, who lives in Hackney, London, with her husband and two children.

Only the Lonely is the first in a series of crime novels, which were originally published in German under the titles *Ich glaub, es hackt!*, *Ach du liebe Zeit!* and *Adel auf dem Radel*, all revolving around the character of Philipp, the accidental detective. The whole series is set in her hometown, Hofheim am Taunus in Germany, where she grew up before relocating to the UK, and the character of Philipp is based on her own father.

She also writes for stage and screen. Her plays are published with Nick Hern Books. She won 'Best Screenplay' at Lift-Off Film Festival's Season Awards 2019 and is co-artistic director and founder of The Fizzy Sherbet Podcast www.fizzysherbetplays.com

More information on www.tamaravonwerthern.com or reach out on Twitter @tamarawerthern

Look out for the next book in the
Accidental Detective series:

In *Silent Night*, Philipp is drawn into a thrilling adventure involving trafficking, old ladies who knit, and mortal peril, both for himself and his loyal sidekick Maschka. And all in the run-up to a Christmas that no one will forget…